THE HITCHHIKER
and Other True Stories

THE HITCHHIKER
and Other True Stories

a book of short stories by
Karl Hiltner

KNIEMST **P**RESS

HUDSON

Kniemst Press
Hudson, Ohio
www.karlhiltnerbooks.com

ISBN 979-8-9852154-1-0
Library of Congress Control Number: 2021923114

*for Clifford L. Schrader, who challenged,
encouraged, and inspired me*

Contents

1.
The Missing Sheep of Coshocton County

In the summer of 1931 CW Baxter and Virgil Taylor began driving to Coshocton to sell potatoes together at the farmers market. It was only thirteen miles to the city, but it took CW two years to convince Virgil to go with him. The county road from Perry Township followed an old Indian path along Sand Fork Creek, then along Moscow Brook, till it split east through the woodlands of the Cherokee Trail, and crossed the Muskingum River into Coshocton. There was a little money to be made selling potatoes and it was one of the few things that Virgil agreed to do together with anyone. It was quite an effort for him to do this because he usually acted alone, especially when it came to consulting with his wife who had become resigned to his cruelty and indifference. He had long ago decided it should be no different than the right to vote for women, which he had never agreed was necessary.

This was before the Baxter barn burned, and before the trouble on the neighboring Heffeifinger farm. There was nothing that could be done when the fire started, as there was no plumbing or electricity until rural electrification went through the countryside during the war. They would lose the barn and then the boy in the space of a few years, but what you cannot know allows you to live. When the fire happened, there was no water plumbed into the house or the barn, and there were no pumps to bring the water up, even if there had been enough water in the shallow creek that ran below the barn.

When a barn or house fire happened it was usually lightning, a dropped kerosene lamp, or spontaneous combustion if hay was put into the barn when it was still too wet. And nothing could be done later about the other trouble, it was just bad luck and you can't control your children. Sometimes when things happen you have no choice but to be an innocent bystander, innocent but damaged, and there was no legal recourse for that. Though the neighboring farms were worked by people as flinty hard as the Indian arrowheads turned over by the plows each spring, when there was trouble you could count on a hand to help, and farming then was hard, dangerous work. At least the Baxters did not lose their home when the barn went. Two years before, after the Von Winkie place burned, the thrashing man who went through all the fields in the area at the end of each growing season, lent them the moveable office he used for his business, to live in until they could rebuild. A person would not demonstrate nor talk about action in those hard years, he would just do.

According to Virgil, potatoes were women's work that came from his wife's garden. It was a free product for him to exploit. His young sons plowed a few extra garden rows for their mother with a one-horse blade, and she did the potato planting and the cultivating with her daughter's help. There was plenty of room in the twenty-acre field above the house for her to put in a few extra rows for the city market. This was no problem for Virgil. He'd get a ride to town with CW, and a trip to the city to get away from the farm for a few days at the end of each growing season. His wife and sons and daughter would do the plowing, planting, harvesting, and cleaning, and he would take the ride to town, and make a little money on the side. Between that, and Roosevelt's WPA Mohawk Dam work, and the engine and machine repair he did, he also leased land for a limestone quarry where the boys did the heavy drilling and the work of setting the dynamite charges to blast out the limestone for the township contracts he was awarded. What with the eggs and cream from his chickens and milk cows, the hogs, the prime beef cattle he sold to the eastern markets, and the wheat and corn he traded for the milling, Virgil made a living off the land, and off of his family from the work of his wife and three children.

Virgil did not like sheep, and the cattle he favored would not graze on fields where sheep were kept. His father-in-law, long dead, had owned the farm that was now his own, and they said he could shear fifty sheep a day with hand shears. Virgil also knew that it was a kick from one of the sheep his father-in-law was shearing that ruptured his spleen and eventually killed him, and he did not favor this work. He did not like to get that intimate with the animals he raised for slaughter. The Baxter neighbor, on the other hand, continued to raise sheep on the farm that bordered Virgil's property. CW told Virgil that he liked the sounds the sheep made, and the fact that they took no notice of you when you walked through the fields where they grazed.

They were neighbors, but it was all business to Virgil. Their conversation over the annual thrashing schedule when the machines were taken from farm to farm, was one of the few times they spoke to each other over the course of a year. The wives might have talked over the fence when their chores allowed, but Virgil rarely would. Trees surrounded and provided shade for both farm houses, and they were nearly a third of a mile apart, and you could not see your neighbor from your house. Virgil would have to walk diagonally all the way across his field toward the road if he wanted to cross his property to speak to CW. He preferred not to take this walk if he did not have to. It suited him to be alone. If and when he spoke, it was business. Neither did he have time nor the inclination for small talk.

The Baxter family had just one son. This meant more hardship for the husband and wife with the work that had to be done. Virgil, on the other hand, would not milk the cows because it also was not man's work. That is what his wife and three children were for. When the boys were old enough, they began to take out the Damascus barreled shotguns- a twelve gauge for the twelve-year old, and a twenty gauge for the ten-year old, but they were not taken out for sport. The boys were expected to get at least nineteen rabbits or squirrels from a box of twenty shells. There were many other examples as well, of the way the work was done on the farm, some more cruel than others.

Silas Baxter, an only child, was good with sheep. His father once took a picture of him while he was holding a lamb, when he was hardly more than a boy himself. It was the only picture they found later when the investigation took place. He stood facing south on the lower pasture above County Road 18. It was a sunny day and he was no more than eleven or twelve years old. You could see the dirt road behind him and the field across the road that led up from a pasture into the woods that crowned the hill. A straw hat with a frayed brim was pulled down low enough so that it shaded his eyes as he squinted into the camera, a long sleeved grayish collared shirt open at the neck, the frayed cuffs rolled up underneath the sleeves past his elbows, stained a grayish color by the sulfur in the spring where they drew their water for the washing, and drinking, and cooking. He wore bib overalls, a folding knife bulged in his left pocket, the right pocket swelled with the faded red bandana scarf stuffed into it. There were patches on the knees where his mother had mended the rough fabric, and frayed denim where the overalls met the tops of his rough boots. The lamb was cradled in his arms, his left hand held the right shoulder of the animal whose head rested on his forearm. Silas' right hand held the hind legs and, and the lamb's rump rested on his wrist.

You cannot always blame a parent for the sins of the child, no matter what the preacher preached at the Perry-Pike Baptist

Church. Years later, what Silas had become, and with whom he had worked and conspired, had changed him from the young boy cradling a lamb in his arms, to another person. Perhaps it had been there all along, a struggle to come forth from inside and be unmasked. No one knows exactly how it happened, how the sheep were moved from the Heffeifinger place east of the Baxter farm. But it was sure they were taken from the field just west of Route 80 hidden from the road by a strip of woods. The field funneled down to a place at the southern most part where the woods were only a hundred feet deep. If you could get the sheep through that natural break, you could lead them across a shallow creek that ran beside the road and herd them into a waiting truck. There were times when the sheep of the Heffeifinger place crossed through that break, so it was hard to say for sure, it was a well-trodden path through the woods. Only that the animals went missing was the certainty. And the gap in the fence by the side of the road where the wires had been cut between two alder posts.

Two young men were involved, only one escaped. The one who was caught went to prison but it is speculated that Silas made it to upstate New York near Watertown for a while, before he crossed the border into Canada. How and why he was mixed up with young Albe Crowtherslee from Coshocton was never clear. Perhaps Albe had talked to Silas' father while he was selling potatoes in the town with Virgil. Twenty sheep seemed a low price for one prison sentence and one exiled life.

It is hard to say what Silas Baxter was thinking, and why he did what he did, and we will never know. Perhaps when the barn burned down, he felt he was somehow at fault, like the child whose parent's divorce, and who blames himself for the family's dissolution. Perhaps he simply saw no other way out from what was inside him. By then there was talk of the war to come, and it was known that he did not want to stay on the farm. All agreed he had been good with sheep, and all that remained for his brokenhearted parents was a picture of him holding the lamb.

2.
Courage

The strip of carpet across the yellow painted floor was not thick and it was not heavy, but then nothing was thick and heavy nor especially comfortable in the third floor two room flat which was home for five people in fifty square meters – parents, grandparents, and the little girl. It was an ordinary postwar flat in a building with no elevators. There were twenty flats in five stories, attached to five more buildings, so that six buildings lined the ulitsa on either side. Nothing was extraordinary for the little girl except, of course, her grandmum's bed, after her grandad died when she was three years old. She missed her grandad, and the gentleness of his affection for her, the smell of her grandad's clothes, the softness of his beard on her cheek, and the sound of his voice when he read aloud the Russian classics and fairy tales. Later, after he was gone, she was finally old enough and strong enough to climb into the bed by herself, no longer prevented by the weight of the casts, and there was now room for her to sleep next to her grandmum, that is, if her father and mother did not notice that the little girl had left her own sleeping place during the night.

During the day in the time when she could not climb into a bed, and there was no space for a little girl between two grandparents, from this room came the sound of a little girl trying to race back and forth from wall to wall, the sound which could not be muffled from the hearing of the woman who lived in the room below. Of course, carpets also covered the walls in the traditional Russian style. These were more decorative than the ordinary ones that partially covered the floor. The footsteps of any other little girl would not have disturbed the resident below, but her footsteps were weighted with the casts on both legs from hip to foot, joined together with a rigid cross member at the knees. Her footsteps fell heavily on the wooden parquet floor, a constant reminder of a child above to the woman who lived on the floor below.

A breech birth is particularly dangerous for the mother, and sometimes catastrophic ending in the sacrifice of the child. During a breech birth labor, the things that must be done are not decisions that can be made by the woman alone, because she will not willingly let go of a child born with difficulty. The men and women who love the woman, and the doctor or midwife attending the birth must assist her and take control of the decisions that attend such a birth. Now with the technologies of modern medicine these situations are almost always known before labor begins, with sonograms and imaging techniques at our disposal. The possibility to move the child to a correct position exists, or the certainty of a Caesarian birth which will save the life and the health of both the mother and the child. But not many years ago this knowledge did not exist, or in certain towns or villages and countries was not yet available. There is danger both to the brain and to the legs and hips with a breech birth, and if you have ever known someone whose legs or hips were damaged, or worse someone whose birth was delayed too long, you know the effect it can have on someone trapped in a body whose full intellect is intact, but whose body is damaged, or whose motor skills are affected because their coming into this world was not fast or gentle enough. There is nothing so sad as the words, "I wish I were never born," from the mouth of someone you love, or even more sadly from the mouth of someone you think you could have loved, if only they had experienced a more gentle birth, or that you had been a better person.

From one side of the room to the other, the child began to walk. Three years of casts on both legs from the hips down, connected with a brace between the knees, and being carried everywhere. Despite all, a child learns to walk and crosses over and over again from wall to table to chair to wall, to chair to table to wall and back and forth again and again. Life finds a way. The movement, clumsy and noisy, a small pounding on the yellow painted wood floor over and over again, and the occasional fall and the picking up.

The mathematician mother spoke to the child within her belly before the girl was born, in the laboratory, and in the flat, on the tram, in the shops, and on a walk through the Lagernyy Sad with its birch trees by the river Tom. After the difficult birth she continued to speak to the child nonstop and carried her in her arms wherever she went. She described every activity performed from morning to night, constant words and instructions, mathematical descriptions, theories, stories, music, poetry, and descriptions of summer breezes. To this child, born with such difficulty, whose legs and hips were harmed when they were pulled free from the womb, the mother spoke about everything from morning to night to assuage the gilt of her daughter's unfortunate birth.

I was constrained in my cast from waist to toe, and could not move my lower body, only my arms and head and torso, and thus my mind overcompensated for my immobile legs. At the age of four months, I began to speak to the amazement of my doctors, and from that time on I have never stopped talking, and still above all others and lovers, I prefer to talk to the woman who began to speak to me before I was born. I could not walk, but my mind roamed as freely as my legs could not. I could speak and therefore think, and I could dream. When I visited the doctors at the children's clinic, the many times to have my legs examined and massaged, they began to call me Radio Masha.

The summer bloomed in Tomsk and by the time I began to talk in the autumn of my first year, my parents sought the care available in a larger city, three days by train and three thousand kilometers west of this Siberian city in which I was born.

Samara is a thousand kilometers south and east of Moscow, possessing a long and beautiful river front against the east bank of the Volga River. It is here that the doctors treated my hips and legs, at the children's hospital on Entuziastov Street, within site of the Semyorka R-7, the first intercontinental ballistic missile which launched Sputnik, the first man-made satellite. Massively unmoving, now a space rocket monument, it was the first rocket capable of orbital flight, perhaps a fitting symbol that I did not understand though it moved me unconsciously. My proud mother was an aerospace mathematician who worked at the city plant, "Progress." After the Sputnik flight the Semyorka R-7 was intended to be a training rocket for the battle crew at the Plesetsk Cosmodrome. I was a breast-fed child who ate calcium tablets to develop the joints of my legs, who listened to my mother speaking mathematical formulas from dawn to dusk in the shadow of the SR-7. And always I was in the arms of my mother

.

A two-room flat. My grandparents, my parents, and me. A not very old place, five stories, no elevator, the third floor, two rooms, fifty square meters, a flat built to the construction plans of Khrushchev for those who had survived the war and those who would be born after.

When you entered to your left, a bathroom with a tub, sink, and toilet. Behind the bathroom on the other side of the wall was the kitchen, with a table, sink, counters, and uncovered shelves. It opened to the living room. The entrance space contained only a coat rack, and a door which led to the living room. Through a door in the living room wall to the right, there was one small bedroom. At night the living room served as my parent's bedroom, and there was also a space for me to sleep. The bedroom was for my grandmum and my granddad. On the left side of the living room was a small open balcony with a solid concrete railing which gave some privacy from neighboring views; beside, above, and below, shielded from the weather by the floor of the balcony above it.

I loved this cozy place, and I had my parents and grandparents to myself. My mother was with me always until I could walk and go to school.

Long before she was born, Aleksandr Rostov and his wife Anna Ivanovna Rostova lived with their son Yevgeny Aleksandrovich on the floor below her parents and grandparents. Now, years later from the flat above them, was the constant sound of the little girl struggling to walk from wall to wall and back again, raising her left hip to swing the left leg forward, the momentum bringing the right hip up and the right leg forward, over and over and over again, from wall to wall and back again. Despite being bound by the cast connected at her knees which spread her legs apart and made movement difficult, her legs and body were in constant motion, her tiny voice a constant cheerful chatterbox without frustration or complaint. She was able to move herself from one side to the other in the world that was her parent's flat.

Lieutenant Aleksandr Rostov fought in the 1st Belorussian Front; an officer commanded by Marshal Georgy Konstantinovich Zhukov in the Battle of Berlin. Marshal Zhukov was respected by the officers who served above his command, but for the enlisted men and peasant soldiers who served below him he was called "The Butcher." Now he stands upright forever on the stirrups of his bronze horse to guard the northwest entrance gate of the Kremlin.

An army nurse who accompanied Marshal Zhukov's troops became Lieutenant Rostov's front wife. There were many unmarried women who traveled with the army participating in active roles in the war as nurses, doctors, administrative personnel; as well as snipers, pilots, anti-aircraft gunners, and forward intelligence observers among many other roles both known and unknown. Many of the army women became front wives amidst the death, destruction, and nihilism which followed them through the war in which more than twenty-five million Russians lost their lives.

Before the war ended, the Lieutenant and his front wife were separated during battle and did not know if either had survived. The Lieutenant returned home without his front wife, and unknown to him she survived and bore his son. But before she made her way back to find him, he had already married a woman with whom he had met on his return, impatient to begin a new postwar life with his new wife Anna Ivanovna, who also bore him a son. Anna Ivanovna learned of the existence of the front wife, and of the son that was conceived before the war ended. The Lieutenant and his new wife had to turn them both away when she finally arrived in Samara looking for him with a child, a son, in tow. There was nothing to be done, and though Anna understood the things that happened during the war, she never forgot that she was her husband's second true wife, not his first, and that she bore him his second, not his first, son. Her husband Aleksandr, the former Lieutenant, was the center of attention in their family. He was handsome, popular, an ex-officer with many friends and many admirers. Anna tried to serve him faithfully, and knew that he loved the son she bore him. Their son Yevgeny Aleksandrovich – Zhenya – lived with them in the flat below where the little girl lived with her parents and grandparents.

I was a happy child, always in the arms of my mother. I tried to move in my clumsy way or crawl by her side when we lay upon the floor of our flat together, or on the grassy fields of a park near the birch forest. When I went to the hospital on Entuziastov Street for a massage to my legs before a new cast enveloped me from waist to toe, my mum later told me that it was the doctors and nurses who christened me Radio Masha because I never stopped talking and asked questions about, and wanted to know about, everything.

When we went to the Birch Grove in Kashtak with its huge trees and carpets of grass, my mum would lay down a blanket so that I could crawl along and smell the grass and the flowers. Nearby was a hostel for families at the Solar Grove, provided by the Party at the end of Irkutskiy Trakt, northeast of the city center. Papa collected birch tree juice which we drank at the Birch Grove. He would make a cut on a tree and catch the sap in a container. It had a strange, sweet, light, sour taste. I loved the taste of birch and the smell of the grass and flowers.

Zhenya's father, the Lieutenant, was a tall, straight man, who always carried himself with a military erectness. His mother Anna was a small woman who was beginning to become the corpulent elder wife, but she was still a refined woman who dyed her hair to a brownish color.

Zhenya was tall and handsome, too, like his father. Women were attracted to him, and others made envious. One night he was beaten in a fight over a woman and sustained a concussion. Both he and my parents were students at the time about to graduate and to begin to serve their time in active service. All were required to go to the countryside to assist in the agricultural harvests organized by the local city administration. Zhenya spent one night at home after he suffered the beating, but on the next day he went to the countryside in an open rough-riding truck with my parents. His condition worsened after he arrived at the barracks to which he and my parents were assigned, and he was unable to work. He died there the next day, unexpectedly, in the countryside barracks of the collective farm.

Anna Ivanovna Rostova never recovered from the shock of the death of her only child. She remembered the first son that was born to the Lieutenant's front wife, and suffered from the guilt and shame and jealousy and superstition that she assigned to both the mother and the son. That both had been the fruit of the Great Patriotic War only intensified the depth of her feeling whenever she saw her now elderly husband in the tunic of his uniform each year on the Victory Day of Remembrance. She was now as childless as the Empress of Russia whose given name she shared

I became a constant in the world in which Anna Ivanovna now lived without her son. I was the sound of a little girl who lived on the floor above, who struggled to walk from wall to wall, raising the left hip to swing the left leg forward, the momentum bringing the right hip up and the right leg forward, over and over and over again, from wall to wall and back again. For three years I was bound by the casts which were connected at the knees to spread my legs and hips apart in order to allow them to heal. The sound of my clumsy steps could not be muffled by the thin carpet beneath my feet in the places where it covered the painted wooden floor. My tiny voice was a constant chatter in her mind, Radio Masha calling, as if I were on a broadcast that could not be turned off.

The Lieutenant and my granddad attended war veteran's meetings together, and represented our apartment building for the Council of the City Worker. It had been several years since Zhenya's loss, and I was almost three years old. They say that when the Lieutenant returned to the flat one night after a meeting of the Veterans of the Great Patriotic War, he found his wife in the bathroom, the water still running from the tap. It was the only way in the only place where she could cover the sound of my steps from the floor above, he later told my granddad. It was no one's fault he would say, but it was finally too much for Anna Ivanovna Rostova to bear on that final evening.

The last thing Anna Ivanovna remembered was the handsome face of her dead son, Yevgeny Aleksandrovich Rostov. She tried to remember the sound of Zhenya's voice, and the day that he was born. Then she drank the caustic soda taken from the kitchen, and she died.

I have no memory of Anna Ivanovna, nor of her handsome son Zhenya who died before I was born, nor of the Lieutenant who fought for the Marshall who now stands frozen in bronze on horseback guarding the entrance to the Kremlin. In the year that Anna Ivanovna died by her own hand, my granddad died as well, and I was freed from the casts that I had worn for my first three years.

I never stopped talking, Radio Masha. But now when my parents fell asleep in the living room of our two-room flat, I was able to walk quietly to my grandmum's room, and climb by myself into her bed. I did not know of the emptiness of other beds. These are among my first memories – my grandmum's arms around me, and of my legs that moved freely beside her.

3.
The Open Window

My offices were on the eleventh floor of the headquarters building. Each floor of the building was split into two sides, between which was the central stairway and elevator shaft. Two thirds of the offices were on one side, and one third on the other. My offices occupied the smaller end of the building which you entered through the door to the right when you exited the steps. I usually walked up all eleven floors, not ten, because you entered the building on the ground floor, and the first floor was one flight up, not the second floor as in America. There were always lots of walkers for the first three or four floors, but for the last seven flights I usually had the steps to myself, and "Jó reggelt!" no longer rolled off my tongue as there was no one to say good morning to again until I entered my offices. Then I would begin the greetings to my staff all over again, in an unfailingly polite atmosphere.

The stone and concrete steps of the central stairways were not steep, and you could take two at a time in cooler weather without becoming overheated by the time you reached the higher floors. The stone stairway of the building was still cool from the night before. But in the summer heat of July and August when the temperature could reach 40°C during the afternoon, it was best to take the steps one at a time and try to remain un-moistened by the heat and humidity in the mostly un-air-conditioned building.

I had never before worked in such a socially cultured environment, where men and women, colleagues and friends, greeted each other with kisses on each cheek in a sincere and kind and yet a very feminine and manly manner. There seemed to be less competition between colleagues, a less aggressive atmosphere where a collegial spirit was in place, where collaboration was easier and where time was taken to be more than just civil. The people with whom I worked were as hard working and efficient and capable as any of my colleagues at home, and perhaps more capable than many. There seemed to be no fear of systems complexities or technical change, at least there was nothing that got in the way of the new management practices that we were tasked to complete. There was a hunger for new methods and new technologies. An intellectual brightness, yet a human gentleness emerged that I had never experienced in the same way. It seemed to me that we were somehow closer to a human nature, closer to the earth, to the gardens and vines that so many had and all appreciated, from the grapes to the wine barrels stored in the lower level of modest weekend houses. It could be felt on a crowded street with a garden in the city, or on the narrow hillside of a weekend house, where we used to pick red currants, mix them with cream for dessert, and call it a picnic after eating fresh peas, peppers, and cheese with a bottle of wine or fresh pressed fruit juices.

I liked to glance at the sign on the double door, identifying my suite of offices before I passed through it each morning. In the beginning it was perhaps out of a frightened pride and fear of failure. In the end it was perhaps the strange excitement of a foreign tongue made familiar.

There were five hundred employees under my care at the beginning when we first arrived, including many grandmothers with grade school educations in a gender skewed function. Most employees had high school educations, and among the many fewer highly skilled and university educated professionals were those who led the factory units for which I was responsible. Among my field finance factory leaders were five men and two women. One man and three women led my office staff of eight in my headquarters suite, fifteen professionals altogether with the factory staffs, and five hundred more reporting to the seven factory leaders.

My first interview was for a secretary. It was my most difficult interview. I found myself sitting across from an unsmiling, tired, middle-aged woman who had a flat, colorless voice that matched the colorless clothing that she and everyone wore when I arrived soon after the Berlin Wall came down and the frontier was opened to the West. Nadia introduced herself and began to read from her CV.

"I was born in Smolensk, Siberia, in the Soviet Union, in 1942."

She was ten years older than me and that would have been even better if the experience had been post socialist. Impossible, since the first free elections in over forty years would not yet take place for another month. She was here, sitting before me only because someone arranged for anyone who spoke English to interview with me. There were not many who spoke English at that time, and I was as unsuitable for her, as she was unsuitable for me. She would not be able to understand what I wanted nor why I was here, and had spent too many years in a traditional office with a bureaucratic manager for whom her main task might have been to greet visitors and bring coffee or drinks. I soon understood that I needed someone from protocol who knew everyone in the building, but someone younger or closer to my age because they would not have worked in the old style for so many years. Growing up in Smolensk, my first interviewee had been given a choice of second languages and had chosen English, whereas in this country all were required to study Russian as the second language. But Nadia was not someone who wanted to understand the changes that were beginning to take place and who would be willing to help to make them happen. That would eventually be Ibolya, a widow not much older than me who had a daughter. She wished to remarry one day and move back to Germany, where as a child she had been settled with her family after the war. She treated me and protected me as solicitously as she would have cared for her own family, and though she was a citizen here, she was an ethnic German, and amenable to a more western outlook.

My stair walking began from the beginning of my assignment. I traveled to the office with one of the managing directors for whom I worked. There was no public transportation from the diplomatic hills in which we lived other than taxis, unless you were willing to walk a half kilometer to a bus stop, wind your way down the hills and cross the river, transfer to the metro, exit and walk another half kilometer to the headquarters building. Soon I would have my own car, a box Lada that I was able to obtain quickly because I knew how to drive a stick shift car. All the other foreign managers drove difficult-to-get automatics imported from Vienna after a lengthy wait. Until I received my Russian kocsi, I rode in with my colleague in his chauffeur driven car, and went up the one flight of steps together to his office on the first floor, before I continued up ten more fights to my own office. Oftentimes, especially at the beginning, we discussed things that happened or issues that we faced as everything was new for us and for the employees of this huge enterprise. Something happened every day. The world was changing. I soon found that it was easier to take the stairway to my office rather than taking the lift from the first floor after meeting with my manager. Taking the stairs became a way for me to physically prepare my body and mind for the day. By the time I reached the eleventh floor, I was ready to look at the sign on the door and enter and greet the people with whom I worked in my four-office suite with a secretary station. Then I began my good mornings all over again, the jó reggelts rolled off my tongue, and there was a kiss on each cheek for any visiting female colleague that might be there for the day from a countryside factory.

It would be months before my family joined me, and everyone in the building knew that I was alone. The wives of the other seven directors had joined them in the first few weeks. Two of the directors had children who finished out their school year with grandparents back home. I was the last hired and the youngest of the directors, all the others had already made their living arrangements before I arrived, and there were no grandparents to take care of my children. So, my wife was unable to join me at the outset of my assignment, and our settling in would be delayed. As the last one to choose appropriate housing and the one with the largest family, I had the most difficult time to find a home that was big enough by what we did not understand then, was only by western standards. Almost all the people here lived in apartments or homes much smaller than what we were accustomed to. Soon we did find a home that would not be finished until after we moved in. It was less than half the size of the home we left behind, with rooms that could not accommodate our furniture.

We lived in a fishbowl. Only one from our group of ex-patriot executives spoke the language. All manner of rumors and suspicions surfaced each day among the employees of our once great national company, whose proud history was nearly carted off and lost, packed into a hundred rail cars that carried all of the equipment east after the war, reparations for the terrible losses incurred by the Russians on the eastern front. Those Russians killed by the Axis powers in POW camps alone numbered almost 15 times the American war dead, with total war dead numbering one hundred times as many Russian versus American losses. All that had been left of the former great company, was what remained hidden and undiscovered in certain basements of the damaged buildings after the war ended. This hidden equipment became the nucleus of the company that was rebuilt after the war. And now some forty-odd years later, the advance on the company would come from the west, not from the east.

In any week you would attend a meeting and despite the confusion of simultaneous translators and a cacophony of discussions, someone would push their chair back from the table, to make an exclamation with a mixture of anticipation, distrust, and fear.

"We have been waiting forty years for this!"

Another week and a newspaper article in the Népszabadság would accuse the westerners of profiting from the takeover of the country's largest socialist company and of setting themselves up in luxury. There was a great misunderstood expectation that the level of wages would quickly rise to western standards, and that the employees would no longer have to "pretend to work, and pretend to be paid."

There was disappointment all around and only endless hard work in front of us all, an impatience to succeed and a realization of the pain that would have to be endured, and an acceptance of the disappointment that many would be left behind in order to insure the survival of the enterprise. It was a grudgingly accepted injustice that those of us who could afford to eat meat at every meal would have to tell those who could not, that health care out of the country was not accessible to loved ones whose treatment was not possible in country. Here, a capable physician's limitation was due to the lack of equipment and technology not available in the east because of funding limitations. Or NATO prohibitions against the importation of advanced computerized equipment still extant in the former socialist republics. There were many such limitations. We labored on.

I soon established good relations with the purchasing organization, whose professorial director was one of the most urbane and cultured men in the company. If you entered his office, enclosed within thick soundproof leather which covered the inner surface of the thick wooden double doors, you were ushered into a softly lit chamber with two windows beside a sitting area for guests, and one window behind an elaborately carved wooden desk. Heavily embroidered fabrics upholstered the cornices from which hung valences which covered the tops of the windows with kick pleats at the corners. The drapery panels covering the windows were drawn aside by gathered swags in ancient-looking gilded silk drop-bead trim. The sitting area lay on top of a worn but elegant oriental carpet that covered the center of the floor which was constructed of parquet hardwood which had aged with a soft patina. The individual tiles moved beneath your feet as they had shrunk in the decades since they had been laid in their geometric patterns. Your shoes glided over this slightly undulating surface and it made a pleasant muted clicking sound as the wood tiles moved against each other underneath your feet. On top of the carpet was a comfortable seating area comprised of an upholstered settee and two upholstered armchairs, facing on three sides the wrought iron coffee table with its deeply beveled glass top. There were formal academic parchments in frames on the wood paneled walls and a few guilt framed lithographs and paintings dimmed from aging shellac. A small metal and crystal chandelier hung from the center of the room. When you looked at the leather-lined doors, they looked like two deeply buttoned upholstered leather seats of two comfortable leather sofas, as if they had been taken from two pieces of furniture and placed vertically on the doors. The room was quiet as the director moved from his desk to one of the arm chairs, a lighted window behind him. In a moment his secretary entered the room with a metal tray holding coffee or tea. Another metal tray already sat on the table filled with bottles of mineral water, glasses, and a selection of sodas.

A young protege of the director attended the meeting. I needed current and historical data on factory purchases, in formats and details which, though available, had never been analyzed in the way in which I needed them. We discussed the data points required, a preliminary format for reporting them, and the time it would take for us to collect the data from our disparate systems. The information for each of our production factories had to be captured in a consistent format so that it could be used to compare not only with our local operations, but against the other global operations of our company.

The business discussion ended, and Zsuzsa was dismissed so that she could begin work on the new project, the first project to be completed for me and our company's new management team. There would be many other requests to follow.

We concluded our discussions, and it was time to talk about history. Here in this country, history was alive, the wave of an unending current from the past to the present. I had never been much concerned with the political or historical past in my professional work experience. For most Americans, history did not extend back beyond the lives of their grandparents. At work it was always about the present and the future, looking back did not go very far, it was limited to a few years of historic documents filed and put into binders on the archive shelves in the office storage closet. After a fiscal year was complete and the final results were analyzed and published, the year was put onto the shelf. But here in this ancient country we talked about generational history, not years or decades, but centuries. Or we talked about wine, and vineyards, or weekend houses, or music from the Liszt Akademia in the Zentrum. And I might be reminded that even some of the wine here in the Tokaji cellars was older than my country.

Not only history came alive with my new colleagues, the present also became immediate in a way in which I was not accustomed to talk, and it was connected with the past in the same way that centuries old buildings housed new families. This way of speaking was more grounded in humaneness, in the simplicity of being, not encumbered only by things of commerce or the consumer marketplace, but the way in which people interacted with each other. There was a kind of wisdom in the way that clothing came off in the spring when the sun returned to the country, as if we shed our protective shells and opened ourselves up to nature, especially the unmarried young women who, when walking with the most brief and sheer clothing on a concrete sidewalk in the city, seemed closer to nature. In the spring, women of all ages carried sprigs of lilacs in their hands. You might pass an old woman wearing a long black coat and a colorless head scarf, carrying a branch of brilliantly hued lilacs. Perhaps it was only possible due to the limits of and lack of income and superfluous prosperity, but this was history and nature present and immediate, which fostered an interest between people direct and unfiltered.

It was as if a curtain fell away between myself and the people with whom I now worked. We met each other face to face and we spoke about life after the business discussions ended. And perhaps that is why Zsuzsa chose to come to my office late one night when everyone else had gone home. She knew, as everyone else also knew, that my family had not yet arrived, and I was living and working here alone.

The lights were off in the outer offices of my suite when she entered into the lighted space in which I worked. To enter it you passed through the entrance way of my staff offices, through a corridor to the secretarial station, and then into a space protectively controlled by my secretary. You had to turn around to enter though the inner door to my office. All of the other offices were in front of the office space I occupied, on either side of the secretarial station. I occupied the large private space in the back, with a range of windows overlooking the distant Carpathian Mountains. An old wooden desk, a long matching wooden conference table, and a modern Bauhaus style Barcelona sofa and chairs surrounded a traditional glass and metal coffee table which completed my office space. My secretary served cold drinks and hot espresso coffee, and the occasional cup of tea to visitors. Zsuzsa knocked on my open door, and asked if she could speak with me, and entered.

She was young, a university graduate who spoke four languages, an engineer by training, smart, self-confident, and ready for the change in business and in government. She had been working for our company, prior to the acquisition, for more than six years, and in her most recent job as a sourcing professional, she had the opportunity to do some limited travel, almost entirely within the country. But she had also managed to cross the frontier border to Austria a few times, and on one vacation had been to the Baltic Sea. She was eager for the changes to come to her country and to herself personally, and she had felt the years pass since she had graduated. She had not yet found a husband nor had yet to bear the child she wanted. Like many educated young women who had not married quickly, who were successful and professional in career positions, she felt with each passing year the fewer and fewer eligible men with whom she could imagine spending the rest of her life. She felt herself growing older, even though she was still quite young. She was an attractive young woman, dark haired with inquisitive intelligent eyes. She was not afraid to meet and hold your gaze when engaged in a business discussion. She projected a self-confidence with a physical presence. She was direct, but not forward. In a meeting you would say she was respectful but eager, civil but not aggressive like some of the young men. She was ready to collaborate. She was not afraid to present her voice and participate. She was an able colleague and one day would become a productive leader, and she worked well with her professorial manager who valued her intellect with an appreciation, strictly proper, of her physical attributes and erdélyi beauty.

"Mr. Hartmann, may I disturb you?" she asked, as she stood in the doorway to my office.

I had heard someone enter the door to my offices but I thought it was one of the young girls who came each night to vacuum and remove the wastepaper. It was Zsuzsa. I hesitated to greet her, as I struggled to remember how to pronounce her name. At the outset of my assignment, I found it difficult to remember the names of new colleagues, but soon Péter had taught me the always consistent pronunciation that you could absolutely be sure of if you knew how a word was spelled. I always wrote the names down at the beginning of each meeting, and I was able to remember Zsuzsa's name, and the way to pronounce it after a moment's hesitation.

"Good evening, jó estét Zsuzsa, of course, come in."

It was late and everyone else had gone home. It was still light outside because we were so far north that the summer nights extended an hour later than the summer days back home.

"Ákos, your director, is a very interesting man," I said of the purchasing manager to whom she reported.

Zsuzsa came into my office.

"I feel like every time I enter his office and sit down, after his secretary brings in coffee and we are very formally made comfortable, I am treated to a discussion as well organized and thoughtful as any presented in a university lecture. He is most unusual. I have never worked with anyone quite like him. I like him very much, and he is very helpful to provide perspectives to me which help me to understand the environment and culture in which we work."

I usually sat behind my desk when I was using my new laptop. In those days, PCs were quite large, and as I needed to travel frequently to work at the remote sites of our operations, I used something more portable. While my machine was portable, it was not small. It would still be two years before modern laptops were permitted to be imported into this non-NATO country.

When I worked with someone, I usually moved to the long conference table which sat in front of my desk. But before I could get up and move to it, Zsuzsa came up to my desk and stood in front of it so she could speak to me directly.

"Yes, he is a good manager and has taught me many things from the time I first began working in his organization. At first, I was nothing more than a clerk. He told me he always sensed my abilities, and I am much appreciative of the development and mentoring he has given to me."

She spoke with an urgency and with a passion and emotion. You could see that there was an intelligent depth to her. She had worked enough years to have a good amount of experience and knowledge of the business. Her languages allowed her to peer outside of the country, unlike some of my colleagues who had never crossed a border and did not speak a world language.

"But Mr. Hartmann, he is of the old school, and he is no longer young. His ways are cultured, intelligent and well-rehearsed, but he is of the old country and the old ways, and I would like to be part of the new world, and I do not want to have to wait."

"I want to work for you, and learn about western thinking and ways of doing things. I am well educated, and I think there are many things I could do for you. You are also the youngest director from your company, and I want to learn the new things that you can teach us here. I want to be part of your organization. I am willing to learn whatever I need to learn, and I am willing to do anything."

She finished what she had come to my office to say, and leaned forward with the intensity of her emotions and desire of change. She placed her hands on my desk and fixed her eyes on mine with sincerity. The light was beginning to fade at the end of the day, reflected from the distant mountains as it came through the windows on the side of my office, and her loose-fitting blouse, clinging only to her shoulders, fell open in front of me. Her body, freed from the blouse, swayed gently as she leaned forward, and my eyes fell down from her face to the movement, then back up to meet her eyes. She remained there and I remained in my seat for what seemed longer than it really was.

She was a professional colleague, but she was also a beautiful young woman, and I moved in my seat to once again meet her eyes and to look at her.

She waited, not moving, except for the gentle movement of her breasts visible before me and trembling from her respiration and heartbeat, and I turned and thought of the glass bowl in which we would both live. I moved behind my desk to the window, stumbling against the legs of my chair, and I opened it.

There was an unexpected gust of wind through my eleventh-floor window as the heat of the day was overtaken by the cooling evening air, and she moved to help me catch the papers that rustled on my desk.

That did it. I had a few moments to gather my thoughts.

As it turned out, she would not work in my organization, but she would become quite successful and in time lead the organization from which she had wanted so badly to leave in her desire to work with me. For the rest of the time that I worked there, she was a special colleague from a special time. We shared a knowledge of what might have been when the world changed around us, but was never, and we both knew we were better off, with what had never happened.

4.
About Life

On the first day of chemistry class, I sat in the second row on the right side of the room. Everyone knew that the teacher was from an elite mid-west school in Illinois. That was foreign to us, because we were the sons and daughters of the depression and WWII. Most of our fathers did not attend a university and most of our mothers stayed at home and still hung out the wash on clothes lines in the summer. When we were just boys and girls, if our mothers did work outside the home, it was usually in what was then considered a woman's profession. They were the nurses or secretaries or teachers or clerks in the shops that were still open on Main Street before the malls came to town. The YMCA was still on the corner of Main Street. The youngest boys had to swim naked during the boy's swim classes, and all of the girls wore swimsuits and giggled as they waited until the pool was cleared, and the boys all ran back into the locker room, afraid of the girls. At least most of us had been afraid of the girls.

Mr. Tailor did not look like the athlete we were told he had been, and he was not yet a coach for any sport. We heard, but it did not seem possible that he had played college basketball, and that he once made eighteen of twenty straight basketball jump shots while shooting around in our high school gym from the top of the key. He was over six feet tall, but he had gained weight and was now much heavier. He had a pallor like cheese, thick legs, and the heavily freckled skin of a red-haired man. His hair was already thinning though he was not yet thirty. He always wore the white lab coat of a chemist, and it flowed about him like a breeze, and it barely covered his girth when closed.

There was a rumor that he was here only one more year, marking time in our small-town school, and that he was going to get a PhD. Most school teachers still had only Bachelor's degrees, and only sometimes a Master's degree. He would be the only doctorate in our school if he ever returned to this small town, and we doubted that he would return. He was an outsider, and different from the others.

He did not speak with an accent, but his diction was different from the other teachers, a more precise speaking style, not loud, but between soft and hard with a richness that resonated from deep in his throat, and sometimes it did not carry to the back row of our class. His voice, though rich, was not powerful, and did not project like a singer's voice did. You had to concentrate and pay attention to catch every word he said.

Most of the boys knew how to use every item in their father's toolbox, watched and helped them with home and car repairs, and many with farm repairs on their parent's or grandparent's farms. The college bound among us knew how to conjugate verbs, translate German or French or Spanish, perform math equations, write essays, give speeches, dissect frogs, perform music, and play sports. But this was the first class in which it seemed to me that we could combine the intellectual with the unseen physical. We would be taught to understand the periodic chart and calculate the height of a soap molecule, to understand the reactions between chemicals, and to be able to predict the outcomes. We were able to discover by means of elementary, logical, and progressive testing, what unknown substances we were given to identify in what became the famous 4-10 test. The successful perfect "10" identification of 4 unknown chemicals given each student by Mr. Tailor, was the challenge of the final test of the chemistry class for the year. Only a few students each year achieved the 4-10 score, and their names were posted on a large display high on the classroom wall. It was Mr. Tailors "Chemistry Hall of Fame". For anyone in a science-based college track curriculum, this was one of the highest honors you could achieve in our high school and it was unique to Craig Tailor's class.

Many years later, after he achieved his PhD and had written his own chemistry text book, I found out that he read at least one book every night, and would perform memory tests for fun, like memorizing the scores of all the World Series championship games in the history of baseball. He needed little sleep, and would work, and read, and memorize late into each night with his restless, indefatigable mind.

These were things we did not know then, or had not yet happened, but we did know he was the only teacher to lead the students, during the one Vietnam War protest ever held at our school. He started the first varsity tennis team, after first learning how to play the game himself in his late twenties. He organized the first high school tennis championship during which, after having just learned to play himself, he nearly won the tournament in a drawn-out match with a sixteen game fifth set, played before tie-breakers were used to limit the games played. He did not like to lose but was gracious in defeat, and still liked to reminisce about that first pre-varsity tournament years later, after his participation, interest, and physical ability had turned to golf.

More than that we did not know about him. He did not live in town, but in the private countryside of a nearby city, and we did not know his family, nor that his wife was a highly educated medical technologist. For years he maintained correspondence with many of his former students upon whom he had made so great an influence, inviting them to his home where he and his wife prepared meals for their visitors. In summers he encouraged players who had graduated to help him coach his tennis team during practice sessions in which they drilled cross courts, down the lines, baselines, and at-the-net volley drills which he particularly enjoyed.

During their college years, he continued to keep in touch with some of his former students, sending copies of the first high school chemistry and literary publication he initiated, with letters penned into the margins of the mimeographed pages in the most tiny, neat handwriting, in notes like this.

> "Thanks for your letter. I do remember reading that book as an undergraduate. It was a landmark in many places and I was moved to obtain it. The description of your college course, and the time you were hitchhiking with the girl was very evocative. The claims your professor made seem extravagant, but the method is apparently highly successful, and I'm interested in the results that will be obtained by further study. I thought you would like to read this issue of our new school literary journal, Chemistron. We'd like to see you when you can get away, and please continue to write, we like to hear from you." Craig Tailor

Thirty years later, my youngest child came home from school one day. There was a visiting science teacher in his class, giving a talk about chemistry and school laboratories, and visual science experiments involving explosive chemicals making interesting reactions. The former teacher was now working for the state to inspect high school science laboratories and storerooms in order to remove dangerous chemicals which had aged, become contaminated, and were now dangerously unstable. To get the attention of the students during his visits, he showed videos he had made of the disposal and sometimes detonation of the dangerous compounds removed from numerous schools. Of course, the explosive disposals were the most popular of his videos, and they were replayed many times.

The students invited to these visiting classes wore name tags, so that Dr. Tailor, now retired from full time teaching, could more personally interact with the young people. He always liked to know the names of his students, even those with whom he would meet only once.

During one of these science visits a young boy raised his hand for a question, Dr. Tailor asked his name, then looked at the name tag, then asked the boy the name of his father. To the surprise of all in the class, and the other teachers present, he said that he had taught the father in his high school chemistry class three decades earlier.

We managed to have two reunions in my home, at dinner around the family table, and we caught up on the years and a lifetime of activity. No longer Mr. Tailor, or Dr. Tailor, he was now Craig Tailor, and a friendship rekindled which spanned a generation. Emails, advice, and games of golf would follow, but we never again played tennis together. One day, after a long period between emails, I received a note from him saying that he had been very ill, and suffered from congestive heart disease. There followed one last selfless note from him before he died, written in the same manner in which he lived his life, expressing hope and optimism for me, his former student, for my family, and for my life, while his own was drawing to an end, and to the memorial service I would attend as a final farewell.

I am certain that there are many in our class who still remember the ripple of astonishment that went through the class like a whisper under our breaths in our first day of chemistry class with Mr. Tailor in September 1968. We did not really know what he meant, but we knew that this was either something strange or special, and at the time most of us thought it was strange. We were to find out that this special class would be unlike any we had already experienced, perhaps any that we would ever yet experience. We were only sixteen or seventeen years old and did not know it then, but Mr. Tailor's class would compare with the best class in any university any of us would later attend, we, the first generation of many of our families to go to college.

On the first day of class, Mr. Tailor wrote his name on the blackboard beneath the five-foot-long yellow slide rule which hung above the chalkboard, the focus point of the classroom that it was to become. And then he did the most remarkable thing as an introduction to our chemistry class.

He wrote on the board in a large chalk script.

"The purpose of this class is to teach about life."

And he did.

5.

The Violin

He told me that the Nazis did him a great favor, when at 18 years of age he said goodbye to his father on Gleis 1 at the Südbahnhof, the South Railway Station in Vienna, Track 1. The Germans had come the year before in another Anschluss, but this time bloodless to the cheers of many in the Österreich. He took with him, as he told me many years later, only a suitcase, a fiddle, and a few shillings he would exchange for dollars, and left behind an audacious promise to his father that he would bring him and his mother to America. One year later in 1940 he made good on this promise. But at that time, standing on the rail siding in 1939, he knew only that his chosen studies would not be permitted, that he would never be allowed to attend university, and that he would never be a musician in Vienna or anywhere else in the greater Reich. He could not have imagined the Theriesenstadt musicians in the camp not yet built in the east, a dangerous fraud of a camp staged for the Rotes Kreutz eyes. His anxiety was for the lack of educational opportunity and work, not for a mortal fear. Sophisticated Austrian citizens could not yet imagine nor accept the possibility, later the fact, of the horror that was to come, because the Germans were nothing if not sophisticated.

Augsburg is sixty kilometers northwest of Munich and five hours by train from Vienna, passing through Linz and Salzburg on the way through Austria. Now there is an intercity high speed express the entire route between Vienna and Augsburg. But in 1939 the way from Vienna through Salzburg and across the border north of the Berchtesgaden lands, and up through

Bavaria from the Alps took several hours longer. Still, even then it was only a long day's journey.

Five years later, in 1944, a now English-speaking Corporal Kurblet would return to Europe with the United States Army and come to this second oldest city in Germany, founded two thousand years earlier by the Roman Emperor Caesar Augustus. He would come to Augsburg not from his native Vienna, but from America. Tens of millions of deaths had already taken place during the war, and millions more would die. His journey would require top secret military training for intelligence gathering, interrogation techniques, and psychological warfare. It would include an improbable army commission, a driver, a rifle, and a jeep.

But if you knew the stubbornness of this diminutive man, the small stature and large intellect, the gift for languages, and the drive to succeed on his own terms, perhaps it would all make sense. A bitterness and a hardness would eventually come to him, a sense of loss unrequited, a man who later was willing to stand up to the giants of his profession and succeed.

"What more could I possibly have to lose, when one has lost almost everything?" he said to me fifty years later.

There would remain in him an emptiness that could not be filled, a place where one could not intrude, a place where only his equally displaced and even more disenfranchised wife who had come from Berlin would understand.

Augsburg is a historical city of peace. During the Augsburg Confession of 1530, Martin Luther's summary of his protestant faith was rejected by the emperor Charles V. It was finally vindicated in the Peace of Augsburg twenty-five years later in 1555. Augsburg was a city concerned less with the inter-religious strife of the Christian religions than the business and wealth building represented by the Fugger family who began as the practical benefactors to German princes and royal weddings, and who still, after five hundred years, continued to be benefactors to this ancient city.

But in late April 1945, the US 3rd and 7th Armies had just taken Nuremberg in a bloody street by street battle, and were headed south to take Donauworth and cross the Danube River on the way to Augsburg. The 7th Army marched on through Bavaria and the 3rd Army swung eastward to Bohemia, the present-day Czech Republic. Both armies ended the war in Austria near the city of Salzburg, a half day west of Vienna where the Corporal's long journey had begun on Gleis 1 six years before.

Corporal Leo Kurblet of the 3rd Army belonged to an Interrogation of Prisoners of War team. He was one of the Army's secret Ritchie Boys, now deployed as part of an IPW team temporarily attached to the 3rd Division of the 7th Army when they crossed the Danube River. They continued south into Bavaria, while the 3rd Army marched eastward into Bohemia. The IPW teams with their language skills had been embedded with the armies since the march across Europe had begun with the 1944 Normandy landings, and would be needed again when the army reached the outskirts of Augsburg and crossed the Lech River.

As the 7th Army approached Augsburg, the city faced the choice of surrender or total destruction. Unknown to the U.S. army, there were resistance groups within the city that intended to reach out to the Americans and attempt to offer surrender. Burghers from cities already captured during the march south had been sent ahead of the army to communicate to the cities that lay within the Army's path. The city elders of Augsburg were told that without a white flag welcome, Augsburg would face the same destruction as had cities which did not surrender to the US Army on its march through Germany.

This industrial city which produced Messerschmitts and submarine diesel engines had incurred the destruction of relentless bombing missions since the first raid of British

Lancasters three years earlier in 1942. Later, a raid in early 1944 destroyed much of the city center, leaving the Rathaus, the City Hall, a Renaissance ruin with only the walls left standing. The 17th century Golden Hall within it was destroyed, a treasured architectural landmark. It would take more than four decades before it was rebuilt. Even then it would not be possible to fully restore it to the beauty of its former gilded treasure.

The Messerschmitt plant northwest of the city near the Horgau Bahnhof lay in ruins, no longer hidden in the forest, and the A8 highway which had served as its runway lay pockmarked and ruined by relentless air assaults. The railroad tracks of the Augsburg Hauptbahnhof, the main railway station, lay like curled spaghetti heaped on a plate beside the main railway station building which remained largely and improbably undamaged. A rubble strewn Maximillianstrasse that led from the City Hall Square passed the destroyed 16th century Fugger Palace on its way to the St. Ulrich and St. Afra Abbeys at the south end of the city center.

The night the Americans arrived at the outskirts of the city, civilian resistance members of an Augsburg group were able to make contact with them, and General O'Donnell delayed the artillery barrage against the city. The next day, German Major General Franz Fehn, who had already been forced to delay destruction of the bridges spanning the Lech and Wertach Rivers, faced the choice of the city's total destruction or surrender. The Freedom Party of Augsburg arranged a meeting between the two Generals, and faced with the overwhelming American forces, Major General Fehn surrendered the city with waves of white flags.

The 7th Army crossed the Lech River and entered the city near the bombed remains of the MAN submarine diesel engine factory complex which lay on the river basin, just north of the fifteenth century city wall which rose on the highest promontory of the city, south of the ruined factory.

The top of the wall formed the Bastion Lueginsland, a place from which to look northward over the land from this highest point in the city. You could see all the way to the hills that rose above the Danube River near Donauworth, some forty kilometers to the horizon. From this promontory, the Augsburgers had watched for the advance of the American armies, the 3rd and the 7th, which split the country into south and southeast territories after taking Donauworth and crossing the Danube. At the Lech River crossing at Augsburg there was no resistance. The bridges had not been destroyed. Between the river and against the north city wall the city canal flowed, contained by the base of the battlement. The canal flowed north and since medieval times powered workshops, factories, mills, and breweries of the ancient city with its complex waterways and six hundred small bridges – more numerous than those that span the canals of Venice. No one could then have imagined a future place which would become a world cultural heritage site, because in 1945 it was a place of danger, death, destruction, defeat, and finally, total surrender.

The Bastion had been heavily damaged when the nearby diesel engine factory was repeatedly bombed, collateral damage which reached to the northern promontory of the city. It was not yet repaired in the three years since the first attack in 1942. Now the 7th Army marched south out of the low lying plain to the north, out of what had once been a poor fishing village separated from the more prosperous city center by Fisherman's Gate. First the army would secure the protection of the Bastion and surround it, then climb to the promontory before heading south through the town.

When the Americans ascended the front of the Bastion a group of German soldiers appeared without helmets and surrendered. They were separated from their officers and interrogated by the IPW teams, and became part of the five hundred thousand captured soldiers that the 7th Army processed on their march through Germany to the war's end near Salzburg.

It had been the end of another exhausting march when one of the American GIs panicked at the site of the German soldiers who were attempting to surrender. He fired into the air, causing a brief skirmish, but without a casualty. The difficulties would have been multiplied many times over without the IPW team's language skills in the partially destroyed city amidst a confusing mix of languages and bombed and burned-out buildings. Civilians and military soldiers converged in a white flag German surrender, though many in the city remained proud of its war effort and the attention that had been given it throughout the war from the Fuhrer himself. Hitler loved the ancient city and had elicited near hysterical fealty from the local population, especially the women, during his inspections of the engine and airplane factories during the war. His appearance at the gala opening of the newly renovated opera hall six years earlier in 1939 had not been forgotten, though now it lay in ignominious ruin.

The western end of the north defensive wall extended from the street level at the Fisherman's gate and east to the city canal. Below the first level of the wall close by the corner of the canal there was once an ancient moat, now long covered and under which would be discovered many years later a Roman fountain embedded with Roman tiles. At the eastern side of the bastion the first address, Lueginsland 1, was now a military guard post, built into the wall on two sides where the wall formed a northeast corner. It was from this structure that the surrendering German soldiers appeared that had caused the brief skirmish earlier in the day. Halfway between the two ends of the northern wall, and against it along an unpaved walking path, three homes had been built a hundred years earlier. These were now damaged and abandoned with holes that had been blasted through in places with shrapnel from the explosions when the nearby engine factory was destroyed. The large central two-story structure was a duplex containing two homes, a separate entrance at either end. The east entrance of the duplex structure was covered with an overhang which looked out over a small garden. The third home was attached on the west side of the duplex, smaller, set tightly against the wall.

After the German soldiers surrendered, there was no more movement on the path along the abandoned stone and mortar homes. All along this wall defensive openings in the obsolete bastion remained, where once soldiers from medieval times manned the ramparts, and now where blast damage from modern munitions created new openings in the old city wall.

Leo's four-man IPW team drove up into a garden space between the guard post and the three damaged homes. The sergeant stopped the jeep, and two officers and the corporal dismounted. The IPW men would make their interrogation reports before they quartered for the night.

The homes built against the wall reminded Leo of a neighborhood he had known in Vienna. a place well outside of the Kärntner Ring, and in an area of weekend houses that had brick walls separating them from the city. He thought of the city he was forced to leave, and the place in Vienna where Wolfgang Amadeus Mozart had lived in a modest pension near the Stephansplatz, within the Ring on Graben Strasse. He knew that Mozart's father, Leopold Mozart, was born in Augsburg and lived here until he was eighteen, the same age that Leo himself had been when he left Vienna. He knew that Leopold Mozart's house in this war damaged city was not far from where he now stood. Leopold Mozart was a violinist. He was the musician for whom the Viennese born US Army Corporal was named.

Leo was drawn to enter the first structure built against the wall, the one with an overhang which looked out onto a garden. He had to maneuver around blast damage and rubble where the wall was broken through. The door, though open, was still intact. He struck a match, found, and lit a candle. On the mantle above the fireplace in a heap of dust and debris he saw an elongated case and moved toward it, knowing what it was and wondering what it was that he would find inside.

Fifty years later he told me it had always been a matter of pride for him that he had worn the US Army uniform. It would mean more to him than the formal tuxedos he wore on the performance stage of one of the world's great orchestras for more than five decades. He rarely talked about it, and only spoke about it to me once after we shared a dinner in a restaurant at the conclusion of one of his concert performances. We retired to coffee and dessert in his neat but modest home. He was a man now at peace after a long successful career, and he spoke briefly to me only once about this one singular experience during the war. The rest of the story of the war and the events of the march across Bavaria were too painful for him to recall. These were things he would not talk about.

He would never drive a German car for the rest of his life, though he liked the Japanese sedan he drove. He liked the energy and brightness of my children who took music lessons in the room next to his at the music academy in which he taught, and the fact that I had lived in Europe, worked near Vienna, and knew a bit about the city where he grew up. I knew what the train station looked like where he left his father in 1939, and I kissed Leo each time we met, the way I kissed my own father, the same way I kissed his lovely wife, who was his treasure, the only one who understood, seinen Schatz.

He told me that there was a violin still in the case, on the fireplace mantel of the damaged, abandoned house that he entered that day on April 28, 1945. As he went through Europe with the American Army, he told me he was never without two possessions – his rifle and his violin. When he opened up the case and took out the Augsburg violin, he realized that it was a better instrument than the one he carried with him into battle, and knowing that if he left it there in that ruined house, it would be lost, or damaged, or burned, as the war continued for him and the 7th Army soldiers in his division. In its place he decided to leave his own violin behind, to be lost, damaged, or burned.

Around the corner on another war damaged street called Frauentorstrasse, Leopold Mozart had lived in the house that bears his name. Perhaps Mozart would have encouraged him to take the Augsburg violin with him, and give vibrations of life to the strings once again. But on that evening Corporal Kurblet was more concerned with resting after the march from Donauworth, and the stress of the interrogations of the captured soldiers that he would conduct, in what was left of Augsburg. He stood amidst the ruins of the war-ravaged home and put the violin back into its case, replaced his own violin on the mantel, and made his way out of the rubble of the home.

The next day, still attached to the 7th Army, Corporal Kurblet moved east to participate in the attack on Munich. But before that attack was to take place, companies of the 42nd and 45th Divisions along with the Corporal's IPW team, were ordered to secure a prison camp west of the outskirts of Munich.

At that time no one knew what it was that they would find in the camp which was named after a 19th century artist colony – a peaceful, joyful, artist colony that had grown to become the quiet, leafy, bucolic, city of Dachau.

6.
Slick and Orl

Orl was a very good man, the best kind really, because he used to be a very bad man.

When he was younger, he was wild and angry, in the way that young men are who drink and who are full of resentment because of the lack of money, or respect, or women. Or the lack of love. My mother could not have known Orl when he was young, but if she had known him, she would have said that he did not have enough love when he was growing up. I do not know about that because Orl would never talk about what he was like before, except to say that he used to be a bad man, a very bad and very angry young man. That he used to be, and that he always would be, an alcoholic.

When Slick and Orl changed clothes in the workshop each morning before they climbed into their trucks, Slick always liked to say bad things to get under Orl's skin. He might pull out a raunchy magazine, a title none of us had ever heard of, and start looking through it while he was standing next to Orl. He always let the pages flop open to the largest two, or three-page view, and describe how the old boy was really putting it to her. His face always lit up at the telling of some old boy putting it to her, his eyes opening wide as he looked up and said it. His skin would start to flush, and if it had not been first thing in the morning before we took the trucks out, and if you did not know for a fact that he wasn't, you might think that he was drunk. But he never was. He would just stand there, slope-shouldered, flat-footed, hips thrust out below his belly, and whistle at the pictures through the space between his front teeth.

From Slick's mouth came words I had never heard before, and have never heard since. These were the most pejorative West Virginian terms for a woman that he could muster, enabling him to talk about women in the most salacious and misogynistic way. He did all this just to have a little fun and to get under Orl's skin, who was now an ordained non-denominational minister who had not taken a drink in more than twenty years. Once Slick's own prurient interest was satisfied, he always tried to take it out on Orl.

Now we all know irritating and obnoxious religious types who are always referring to God's will in the most saccharine, cloying manner, but Orl was not one of these. Orl never blamed God's will for any of his sins, they were all on himself, he would say. But he did credit God's will for reforming himself from a drunken bare-knuckle brawler to the man he strove to be today, who despite such taunts, no longer carried a chip on his shoulder, ready to roll up his sleeves and start a fight. Orl simply shook his head at Slick, and told me not to listen to such nonsense. Then he would tell Slick that he felt sorry for him and would pray for him. That always deflated Slick's balloon, and he would slink away to the day's work, crestfallen at his inability to get a rise out of Orl. He was no longer Slick Silkie from the holler. Silkie was his real name. He was as empty inside as the hills from which the coal had already been stripped, and was a slick as his nickname, which was the only name he used after he was all grown up.

Both men were hard and proud workers, and if there was any trouble, they would rush to help someone in need. One day Ross, a young high school teacher who worked at our shop in the summer, tried to remove a semi-truck tire himself to fix a flat. One of the steel rings exploded off the rim with a crack like a gunshot, because Ross had not deflated the tire before he tried to break the bead seal. He had been standing on the tire treads with the sledgehammer, banging away like he was chopping wood, his shirt off to show us all how strong he was. If any part of that ring holding the bead in place had let go and hit him in the head, it could have killed him. He was lucky that no one got hurt, but when Orl and Slick came running to help, there was no degree of separation between the three of them. It was everyman to help the other in need.

The owner of our company knew a widow in town. Her late husband had been a business associate, and the owner and their wives were friends. They had known each other since the war and maintained their friendship over the years. The widow was younger than her late husband and she was a natural beauty, but she was emotionally fragile after her husband's death. When she needed to talk, she visited the owner's wife. If she needed help with her car or her home, the owner and his wife always offered to help her. When she needed gas for her car, she came to the shop. Our gasoline pumps were installed mainly for the use of our own trucks, but a few friends of the company still bought their gas from us for their personal cars. It was my job as the young man hired for the summer, to pump gas for the occasional customer, and whenever the widow came to the shop, we all took notice.

If she came in while I was atop the five-thousand-gallon road oil tank filling Orl's truck and unable to climb down, Orl would help her at the pump. He always tipped his hat to her, the gentleman he now truly was. He would fill her tank and put her at ease with his politeness and easy conversation. Were Slick there instead, a lewd comment to himself always followed under his breath.

"I'd like to have a piece of that there...", he would begin to say.

His voice would trail off, and a low whistle would pass through the space between his front teeth, then he would shuffle over to help the widow at the pump.

If anyone else was there with Slick, we would not let him help the widow. If he did, he never tipped his hat to her as Orl would. Instead, he would walk to the car slowly, take his hat off, hold it in his hands in front of him like an obsequious hired hand to a boss, and meekly pump the gasoline for the widow. There would be no conversation, just the quiet work of a humbled man before a beautiful woman. She humbled us all with her beauty. For Slick, though, the interaction with her became a shy, silent, bluster-less self-rebuke of his own coarse character.

There was the day though, when the widow needed help at her home for one of those things that always happens if you own a home. A clogged drain, a stuck or broken window, a light switch that needed replacing, or some such small repair that needed to be done. I was the one who pumped her gas and filled her tank that day, and after I put the filler-cap back on the fuel tank, and let the license plate flip back up to cover it, she asked me if I could drive home with her to help her with a problem. It was not an unusual request. I often helped at the owner's house, too, with yard work and the occasional task at his home. For a high school boy just about to enter college, it usually meant cold milk, sandwiches, and fresh cookies for the work that needed to be done.

I went into the office to get permission to help the widow, and waited until the office manager got off the phone. He was taking down an order. I could see out through the windows of the office to the widow's car where she modestly waited. Inside the office were two desks facing each other and pushed together, one for the owner and one for the manager. Several chairs stood against the wall. The only other furnishing in the office was an old refrigerator which kept the lunch buckets cold for the drivers and me. It was filled with an assortment of cold sodas, and a tin cup into which you tossed a dime if you wanted to drink one of them.

The widow drove a late model Cadillac sedan, the only other Cadillac that came to our shop except for the owner's black Fleetwood. Her car had a vinyl roof made to look like a closed convertible top, leather seats, and enough chrome to let you know that it was an expensive car. The manager told me to get a clean towel from the workshop to cover the seat before I got into the car. I brushed off my work clothes and slid onto the front passenger seat for the short drive to her home.

I sat at the kitchen table while the widow made coffee for herself and began to tell me what it was that I needed to do. She seemed sad that day, but she was usually very quiet even at the shop where she knew all the men who worked for the owner. She put her coffee on the table and described in detail the repair that needed to be completed and put several cookies on a plate and poured a large glass of milk for me. She began to move to sit down across from me, but hesitated and then moved back and stood behind me. She put her hands on my shoulders, and as I sat frozen in silence I heard her emit a quiet gasp as she brushed her hands against the top of my head. I could feel the warmth of her sorrow for just a moment, then she sat down without a word on the other side of the table facing me.

"I'm so sorry," she began.

A silence stood between us for a moment as she raised her eyes to meet mine.

"I still miss my husband so much. You see, we had no children, and it would be so much easier if we could have had a daughter or a son like you."

"Please forgive me."

I tried to think of something to say and somehow it came to me easier than I ever thought it could.

"It's OK," I said. "We are always glad to see you when you stop by the shop. It always makes the day a little bit nicer for us, and we are always happy to help you."

After the repair was finished, she drove me back to the shop. It was the end of the day, and Slick, Orl, and Ross were still there cleaning up. They watched me get out of the car as the widow thanked me with a wave of her hand and drove off.

When I came into the shop, Slick and Ross kidded me, and Slick asked me if I had, "put it to her." Ross laughed. Orl glared at both of them, growled and clenched his teeth, and the shoulder muscles tightened around his thick neck.

Orl, the reformed alcoholic, the lay preacher, and the former bare-knuckle fighter was the only man who always tipped his hat to this beautiful woman with kindness. He knew, and he smiled, and then he tipped his hat to me.

7.

Vite Vite, Plus Vite!

Agard Davad was from Goa, and he had the most beautiful suits and shirts of any of us on the foreign service team. His clothes were better than the clothes the CEO wore. He wore them with a definite flair and style, and it seemed to come from him alone and not from his wife's urging, even though she was also the best dressed woman of all the wives, with the most beautiful clothes, and with the most glamorous style of wearing them. Davad was the most ambitious of us all, acted and managed with the most direct and confident style, which was a large part of his persona as well. He had the most specific work plans and implementation schedules of any of us in the other functions, and seemed to be the best manager among us. He was capable of managing his team without taking off his coat and rolling up his sleeves like the rest of us had to do in the heat and lack of air conditioning. For him there was no necessity to dive into the details in shirt sleeves with his team to try to figure things out. Maybe it was inevitable because of the function he was put in place to manage, Information Systems. He always seemed to know where the information was, and he definitely seemed to have a system to be able to find it, to fix it, and to use it.

His clothes and his shoes were the best I had ever seen, except, or at least on par, with the suit and shoes I once saw John Leach wear at the Company's Education Center. That was at the end of a day after all of the training courses were finished. We heard the Bell Ranger Turbine 206L-1 Long Ranger helicopter fly into the compound and land, churning the air outside the classrooms and announcing John's impending visit.

We all rushed into the hallway outside the class rooms to get as close a spot to him as possible when he made his entrance to address the classes at the Center. This truly was one of the best things he did in those years, and he was without question a leader, whether you agreed with his business goals or not. He allowed questions up close and unfiltered from those bold enough and confident enough to address him, but he did not suffer fools. I stood safely behind his left shoulder with as innocent a look on my face as possible. I could not help but notice the fineness of the weave of his suit coat, and the softness and perfection of the leather of his shoes. I did not ask a question, but I could see the answer in his clothes and in his shoes. I'm sure that if Agard Davad had been in my executive management class that day, he would have been square in front of Leach, and would have gone toe to toe with him, not only with his questions and the answers and debate, but with the warp and weave of his own suit, the crispness of his cuffed shirt, and the quality of the leather and the polish on his shoes.

When Davad pulled on the cuffs of his shirts, the monograms always appeared perfectly placed just beyond the sleeves of his coat. I have never been able to do that, but I did not have monogrammed shirts so it was a moot point for me. When one of our local colleagues pulled on the cuffs of his shirt, it was usually to remove a fraying thread from the edge of a fraying cuff, and most times there was no coat to bother with. But Csákó István had more redeeming qualities other than how well pressed his shirt was, or whether the cuffs were frayed, so we never gave him an embarrassingly hard time about it. Not even when he came to the office prepared for one of our business trips with a cardboard box from the shipping department for his clothes. He did not yet own a suitcase that was as presentable as his frayed cuffs, and it was never a problem during the monthly two-day trips to our countryside factory manager meetings. No one ever played a practical joke on him and tried to empty his clothes box which did not even have a lid, just the kind of flaps that were folded over and taped for a shipment.

"Do you Americans always suit coats wear to work?" he once politely questioned me, "egy kérdés, legyen szives, a question, please"

And another time.

"Do you every day eat meat?"

Zinga worked in the Protocol department. A young woman, she was the most beautiful in the headquarters building, she was lovely to behold. She was only nineteen years old, did not yet go to university, and when she wore one of her sweaters all of the men and especially the drivers spent as much time as possible in the lobby by the Protocol counter behind which she sat, always with the most correct posture. She knew how to lean forward and look into your eyes if you asked her a question. She instinctively knew just how much of an angle to put into her answer, as she leaned forward into it. I was very fond of her simply for her beauty, and the innocence of the way she expressed it. She knew I would never attempt to do anything about it, because she was the niece of a colleague with whom I worked. My colleague, her aunt, asked me one day if I thought Zinga was attractive, and of course I had to agree that she was. She must have said something to her because from then on Zinga liked me, and knew she was safe with me because of her aunt. She always understood with whom she was safe and with whom she could not trust. I fell into that first, harmless category. But it did mean that I could openly enjoy her beauty and attraction without fear of making a fool of myself, since she was only half my age.

We were part of the first major joint venture behind the former Iron Curtain. There was no infrastructure for expatriates if you did not belong to a foreign embassy, nor have a diplomatic passport. There were no tourist offices nor social services for those who did not speak the language. There was no provision for medical or hospital care for foreigners. If you needed care you had to know someone who knew an English-speaking physician, usually an immigrant, in a hospital who was willing to register you under an assumed name. Medical services were paid with cash and a generous tip. Neither did any of us have a company car yet, it was one of the things that took time to figure out, just like getting a telephone. If you took a house without a phone line, it might take eight months to arrange one, so we were told not to look at homes unless they already had a phone. If there were no lines yet installed on an entire street, you might not be able to get a telephone for over a year, or never.

We did not know how to go about getting cars at first, unless it was one of the Comicom Russian or Slovak cars, or in the extreme an East German Trabant. I was probably the only director who had even been in a Trabant, but that was because one of my colleagues whose family owned one, had once given me a ride when I went to the countryside near Gyöngyös and the Mátra to look at the grape roots they grew for vineyard customers. It was a surprisingly good car, a new model with a 1.1liter VW engine. But it was still a Trabant.

It is astonishing how efficiently the needs of a director like Davad can be understood and fulfilled, and soon his Volvo was on order. The cars for the other directors were quickly ordered in mass. But on this day, there were still no Volvos, and Davad offered me a ride home with his driver and his box Lada, a car which will always be endeared to me, not because of its automotive capabilities, but because of the people with whom I came to know for whom this car was a luxury available only to the former socialist management class. In fact, I would have no driver assigned to me, and as yet I had not been assigned a self-drive car. I was glad to get a ride to the Panzio Apartments where we all lived, while we waited for permanent housing to become available.

Davad called down to Protocol and ordered his car and driver to be ready for the ride home. János, his driver, was in the parking area for the company cars between the headquarters building and one of the manufacturing halls. All the drivers waited in this inner courtyard during the day, on-call if any of the directors needed their cars. It was across from the entrance to the canteen, and therefore close to espresso coffee and the WC. All the drivers were constantly cleaning the glass of their cars, using rags which were always gray from use but which never seemed to streak the glass.

They were always polishing the windshields and cleaning the mirrors. When a driver was called, he would bring the car around to the front entrance of the building, and wait for the director by the curb. He would continue to polish the glass while he waited, always wiping down something on the car. In those early days there was so much pollution in the air it was necessary to polish the windshield frequently. There was always a cloud of exhaust fumes in the air, especially from the two-cycle engines of the old Trabants and the plumes of smoke from ancient diesel trucks. There was always an oily residue on the windscreens if they were not kept clean. That is why the rags always looked gray, and when the glass was wiped and polished it left no residue, as the oily pollution evaporated off the glass when it was wiped dry.

János was waiting for us as we exited the lobby of the building. One of the employees whose only job was to open and close the doors for visitors and directors led us outside. The door minders would soon be among the first employees to be let go, as we were now a profit based joint venture, not a state-run employment social enterprise. I would also soon issue instructions to my own organization to cull the weakest, the least skilled, and the least educated from my over-employed staff.

Agard was in fine form, gave a once over to Zinga and the other protocol greeters, with a wink to her and a wave of his hand to the others. He always seemed to have the air of a senior executive posthaste to an important engagement. After all, he was going home for dinner at the Panzio, where we had all made our temporary living arrangements. I smiled when Zinga leaned over with the gift of her figure and said hello to me as I passed by the protocol desk, and I followed Agard out the door.

The evening before, Agard played the part brilliantly as I dined with him and his wife in a small quiet restaurant near our Panzio residence. I ordered a meat dish with wonderful fried potatoes, while he and his wife had lovely fish, insisting that the head be intact when brought to the table. They knew just how to use the fish knife to expertly remove the flesh from the bones. For dessert I had a sweet Hungarian confection while they ordered a plate of cheeses, a dish I had never before seen ordered for dessert. There were many important things like this for which I was not yet properly educated, and both Davad and his wife were well aware of my shortcomings and needs. I think it delighted them to be able to help me understand many important things about which I needed to become aware, if I were to become a proper guest and more importantly, a proper executive in this European country.

But now I trailed Agard as we left the building, and with another wave of his hand he summoned János who was waiting at the curb. János pulled the car up and opened the front seat passenger door for him.

"Mr. Agard, sir," he said to Davad, while I climbed into the back.

We headed south on the Váci út along the mighty Danube River with Davad firmly in control, sitting regally in the front passenger seat of the well-worn box Lada. His French cuffs were perfectly tailored from the sleeves of his coat, the gold links just visible inside the edge of his sleeves as they held the cuffs together, his hands poised confidently on his knees. He sat ram-rod straight, and moved unconcerned with the jolts of the rhythm and motion of the car as it maneuvered around the dips and crests of the patched and pitted streets, his movements as fluid as those of an expert equestrian. We chatted, and as he talked, he continued to look straight ahead. He turned only his head as the car moved across intersections to make a left or right turn, and he spoke in an animated manner to János whenever he made a sharp turn, or a crisp upshift, or overtook another car.

"Bravo, János" he would say, especially when the engine of the old Lada screamed near the limits of its RPMs as he maneuvered it through the city streets.

We crossed the Danube on the Árpad bridge and went south on the Pacsirtamezö and Lajos streets, through Margit körút and Szilágyi Erzsébet, and began to climb into the Kútvölgy hills of District 12 until we were at the base of Csipke út, a road that would be illegally steep if it were in the United States. Csipke út led to the Panzio on Cinege Road, with its furnished apartments, rooms, and the small restaurant on the ground floor. They served breakfast, sandwiches for lunch, and simple dinner meals for the guests staying there consisting of salads, hearty soups, stews, and meat dishes. On the way to the Panzio we passed a small shop selling flowers, the virágok that Agard sometimes stopped to buy for his wife. He liked the sound of the word for flowers, and the way letter r rolled from your tongue. Other shops repaired cars, and still others had begun to sell small household items. These small private shops, called Kft's, began to appear everywhere in the city. The neighborhoods were quickly adjusting to the new politics of acceptable materialism, especially in the districts where the foreigners, the wealthy, and the diplomats lived.

Now we had driven through all the heavy traffic, now we were in the Buda hills, and the streets were narrow and badly maintained with little traffic. Those who walked trudged slowly up the steep roads and paths, mostly older women with bags in each hand, balancing them like ballast trying to pull them to the pavement. There were no buses here in this neighborhood as the streets were too narrow and too steep for the smoke spewing diesel vehicles. You either had to walk up from the thoroughfare below the neighborhood, or down from the thoroughfare which surrounded the neighborhood from above. Once you escaped from the smoky fumes of the city's public and private transportation systems and made your way here, the air was fresher and cleaner, and you could see across the hills if you were able to afford a balcony high enough to give you a view.

At the base of the final hill that led up to the Panzio, János stopped the car before crossing the intersection. Agard Davad placed his hands on his knees. His hair remained perfectly coiffured, his cuffs were perfectly aligned with the sleeves of his suit coat. From the front passenger seat of the motionless car, he raised his hands like a conductor, while the car sat idling at this final crossroad.

The driver, Kovács János, waited at the intersection like the concertmaster of an orchestra ready to play. His right hand was on the gearshift, his left hand gripped the steering wheel, and his eyes watched both the music on the street and the conductor sitting beside him. Davad – as if he were wielding a director's baton – began to make a sweeping motion forward and back with both hands, opening his fist and extending his fingers palms down as he moved his hands forward and up, and closing his fingers as he drew them back and down as if he were rowing a charging boat. And János began to play as he engaged first gear and let out the clutch.

"Vite, vite!" Agard commanded.

"Fast, fast!"

He moved his hands upwards and back emphatically as the Lada shot forward and began climbing the hill before us.

"Vite, vite!" he cried more loudly.

János shifted gears, and the Lada planted its rear axle to the road as we climbed the hill, and the engine roared. Higher and higher and higher we went.

"Vite, plus vite!"

"Fast, faster!" Agard demanded, and János bore down on the accelerator, the gear shift, and the road.

"Vite, vite, plus vite!" Agard finally shouted out.

The Lada barely gripped its tires to the road and began to slide around the corner as we approached Cinege út. The dust kicked up from the road, and the exhaust billowed out behind our car which responded to the perfectly manicured hands of Davad, and the exhortation to move fast and climb the hill at full throttle.

I did not understand why Agard Davad chose the French language for this performance, it just came out of him. It was his sentiment of the moment. It was who he wanted to be. At that time German was the second language, and the "schnell, schneller" of it in German seemed more tangible to me, and closer to the truth of "gyors" which was the Hungarian word for fast.

To this day I can see Agard's hands, and the back of his neck, the thrill of his voice, and János slapping the gear shift into place and slamming his foot to the accelerator. I guess it did not really matter what Agard Davad had said, or how well he had said it.

Much later, after Davad was gone and I remained there, and when I could speak some Hungarian, and János could speak enough English, we talked about what had happened on that drive home to the Panzio years before, so soon after we had arrived as foreigners in his country. I believe now that Kovács János had understood all the things that Agard Davad, Director of Information Systems, was truly saying, and so had I.

8.
Little Girl and The Boy Who Could Not Swim

St Johns Court was elegant, but it had the appearance of never having been maintained over the years since the court was built in 1879, a street that had not changed since a famous Indonesian explorer lived there as a child at the turn of the 20th century. The house on the Court was an old manse which stood on a leafy street, though it now had the external appearance of being just another non-descript large brick row house. It was on a one block street bookended by 1st and 2nd Avenues west and east, and between E.9th and 7th Streets north and south. When you entered this home through the front door, a large vestibule led into the central hallway. The sitting room was on your left. The end of the wide hallway opened to a banquet sized dining room, unless you ascended the stairs to the right. Beyond that, filling the entire back of the house, was the kitchen. A large formal library was at the top of the stairs, a richly paneled room with a fireplace and French doors which led to an adjoining room, and a balcony enclosed in leaded glass windows. The bedrooms were on the upper floor above. The main bedroom faced the street, with a large old-fashioned bathroom attached to it which still held an ancient claw-footed tub and the original black and white ceramic tile floor.

This is where the child sat happily in a chair, which I held tilted back against the tub while her mother washed her hair and rinsed out her curls, a mother and child happily together as I knelt protectively by their side. I played the child's "uncle" when her husband was away on those evenings when she did not feel safe to be in the large home alone. It was in the vestibule where I told her one morning, bicycle in hand, that we would have a strange life together, before I pedaled home to shower, change clothes, and catch the 6 train to work.

The kitchen was commercial in style, fully furnished for the large, elegantly fading home where serious entertaining once took place. Large metal pots, heavy butcher block surfaces, a multi-burner gas range top, above a three-oven base, and a large pantry filled the cooking space. A door opened to the small garden in back. It was divided in two by a row of brick pavers and an old-fashioned limestone fountain, which had not been used for decades. Beyond that stood the wooden fence and locked gate, which led to the alley behind. The kitchen was a place for serious cooking and the assembling of things to eat that she seemed to know how to do naturally. It was not something she learned from her mother nor not, much later, from her mother's companion. Her father, now long dead.

His award winning interior industrial designs were the only things he left behind, she told me, along with the memory of a rowboat she paddled with him when she herself was a little girl. It was now many years since he killed himself, she said. Now his memory was embodied in the design and construction of the new wing he had helped build, which was attached to one of the city's old elegant public libraries, a modern receptacle as much for entertainment as it was for knowledge. In a perverse form of educational publicity, whole rows of book stacks moved in and out like an accordion bellows, which allowed room for an educational auditorium which featured mostly popular attractions which required no reading or research.

There was a constant stream of friends who came into and out of this great open home, always welcomed without invitation. Those less intimate were the invited guests. All were greeted with a "Hello, darling!" welcome. There was always something to eat or drink, and interesting places from which the guests had come, descriptions of the work they performed, and interesting places to which they would go after their visit. Sometimes it seemed as if her Italian sports car idled constantly on the street, ready to go at a moment's notice, able to be parked wherever it was necessary with the governor's plate thrown visible upon the dashboard. Many times, he remembered that car sliding to a stop on the street in front of the main entrance to his office, the door flung open to him, a picnic lunch on the passenger seat as he exited his office for a mid-day rendezvous with this beautiful woman, his colleagues agape on the sidewalk, left behind.

"Where do we want to go today, darling?" she would smile to me, and say hello to my colleagues standing beside me, while she revved the engine impatiently.

But sometimes love is only recognized and finally realized when it is too late.

Hers was a comfortable lived-in home, if a bit shabby from the many un-remodeled years, a place where real living was done, with constantly changing lives of the arrivals who included young business minds, middle-aged professors, graduate students of the professions, journalists, and other gentle beings. Her circle of friends included transferred academics from southern universities who had escaped to the north, but still desired the genteel greenery of a quiet, leafy, shaded, pseudo cul-de-sac, preferably one which was contained within an elegantly named court. These homes were outside of the expanding core of universities, medical centers, and financial centers of the lower city. Life on the court enabled you to feel alive, to breathe new life into this old town. Though you lived in proximity, you knew you needn't cross to the other side from the protective cocoon of your one-street manse.

A friend of hers lived in the River Shore Towers, with a community pool between the two buildings. On summer days it was a fine place to bring children because most of the people who lived there worked during the week, and it was quieter than on the weekends when the adults would congregate and were less tolerant of splashing, noisy children. One day we brought her daughter and the young son of another friend to the swimming pool. Before she and I had put our things on the chairs by the poolside, her daughter jumped into the water and began swimming to the other side and back. The boy stood as far as possible from the side of the swimming pool. He was afraid and did not want go near the water, and his pale skin looked like it had never been touched by the sun.

I entered the pool at the shallow end, came over to the edge of the pool and stood there in the water waiting for him. The little girl repeatedly called for him to jump into the water to play with her, but he was afraid because he did not know how to swim. His mother was a single mother, alone, and he did not know who his father was. He was afraid of men, undecided about me, and very afraid of the water. His mother had little time for him when she was not working, and she had other issues as well, physical and mental, with more than one addiction. The results of which were all summed in her son as he stood by the edge of the pool, and would not come into the water.

Finally, I came out of the water and gently took his hand, and I asked him quietly if he wanted me to carry him into the water, and give him a swimming lesson.

"Only if you never let me go!" he said quietly to me, with fear in his downcast eyes, trembling though he was not yet wet, even though it was very warm in the sun.

As I lifted him into my arms and entered the pool on the steps of the shallow end, he clutched his arms tighter around my neck, with each step I took into the pool. His shyness made me laugh, and I tried to make him feel safe as I held him securely in my arms. The little girl and her mother swam over to us and gently encouraged him, trying to allay his shyness and fear of the water.

He was as stiff as a board as I tried to unfold him and place him on the water's surface. He arched his back to try to keep his face as far away from the water's surface as possible. He was rigid with fear. I was told later that his mother had not wanted the child though she kept him, but he was not a happy, secure, well-cared for little boy. Men came to visit his mother in their one room apartment, separated from the boy by only a fabric hung across the room, the sounds of rough sex and drinking and smoking not separated from the child. He was as afraid of the surface of the water in which I now tried to teach him how to swim, as he was of the men that his mother brought home and the sounds that his mother and the men made while he lay in his bed, listening. He did not know if the men were hurting his mother, and he was unable to escape from the sounds as he lay in his bed on the other side of the room. Now as I tried to hold him on the surface of the water, he was overcome with panic and could not trust that I would hold him safely and not let him go. The water and the men were more powerful than he. He did not have to understand this fear, it overcame him.

We did not stay long in the pool. I never let him go, and only once did his face touch the water. But when once it did, he screamed and climbed onto me like a frightened kitten, as far out of the water as he could claw onto my hips and shoulders, and he would not let me put him back into the pool.

Later, the marriage ended, and the elegant but careworn house was sold. The new street on which mother and daughter lived was not a leafy court and the home was not a manse. Boarders now, not owners, they rented a divided home from a hoarder, you could hardly move through the downstairs where the eccentric landlord lived. He kept to himself mainly in the kitchen, where it might be possible to find a chair or two partially uncovered, along with at least a small space on top of the kitchen table, enough space for a glass or a cup among the things piled high on top of it.

She would rent, and eventually own this hoarder's home, and began to work first on the upstairs bedrooms and baths. She was harder now after I had gone, and stood hands on her hips, a flannel shirt unbuttoned in the heat to bare her torso, barely covering herself as she gave instructions to the workmen who buzzed around her like worker bees around a queen. A kind of sadness replaced the joy of the one house to the other, friends who no longer came and went, to sit together at dinner, to discuss, to debate, and to empty flasks of wine which no longer sat upon the table.

Finally, my last visit, arriving at night after a long flight when the little girl was already asleep, the sheets were laid out on the bare floor to become my bed. I awoke in the morning to her mother's final embrace, a confusion of loose bed coverings and intertwining. When the child awoke, her mother called out to her to tell her I was here at home, and she came running down the hallway and into my room, as I covered her mother and myself with flowing fabric. She called out to me, "Uncle, Uncle, Uncle!" falling fast together with us in my lap, her arms around my neck, her face pressed against mine, holding me as tight with her arms, as the boy who could not swim.

9.

The Message

The Roberts Sand & Gravel Company, called S&G by everyone, was just across the river south of town. A gravel pit was formed there in the bend of the river where it had been deposited after the glaciers scoured the area in the last ice age. When the superhighways came through during the Eisenhower administration, its business boomed as it supplied the sand and gravel used by local concrete companies. Until then, the sand and gravel business served the concrete market for small customers, municipal needs, county road building and maintenance, and occasional construction projects for the high skill shops and plants in the town. That was when all small towns had factories run by U.S. conglomerates that still invested in this country, paid good union wages with benefits, and were served by the boys and girls who took classes at the vocational schools or graduated from public high schools but did not go to college. Not everyone was expected to go to college in those days. It was an accepted fact that college was not for everyone, and you could make a living and raise a family with a decent blue-collar job. In church on Sunday mornings, the drivers, machinists, and laborers sat side by side with the office workers, managers, doctors and lawyers. No one thought it was above or below their class to do so. There was no need to talk about it, and there were still no gated communities.

However good it seemed to most, it was accepted too, and never talked about, that all the minority residents lived on one side of town in a separate neighborhood that was not easy to drive through because it was a dead-end neighborhood. The streets led into and out of, but not through the neighborhood. If you did not live there, you still believed that it was a de facto, not de jure separation. I guess that means we were living our lives by a 50/50 morality creed, as we were right about one thing and wrong about the other. There was no shame in living by the strength and wisdom in your hands, and we did not yet admit or think much about the shameful other aspect, that the color of the skin on your hands still made a difference.

There were only two men in the office at S&G, and you could tell by the parked cars who was who. Richard Blake, the office bookkeeper drove a Ford, and even though his car was never more than a few years old, it was not the brand-new Buick Roadster that John Roberts drove, nor the new convertible Pontiac that John drove on summer days.

The truck drivers parked out back by the shop where they kept their lockers, and where they sat when they were in the plant during lunch time, or waiting to go out on a job. Their personal vehicles were old trucks or rusting sedans which they drove to work, even though they made good union wages. These were cars or trucks that could go out on a job if need be and not get beat-up for the first time if they were new. When they always did get beat-up, it was okay. These were not the urban trucks that people drive today with aluminum wheels and four-wheel drive with luxury interiors. These were standard pickups with plastic covered bench seats impervious to oil and grease. They all had three speed stick shift transmissions and were never four-wheel drive. The shift lever came up out of the flat floorboard, and was two feet long with a hard plastic ball on top. Air was standard. If you wanted it, you rolled down the windows. You opened the winglet in the corner of the front window by pushing it out by hand so that the air blew against you. You could swing open a side vent in front of the door near the floor if you wanted air on your legs.

Most of the men did work on the side, or tended farms when they were not at work at S&G. This was a small, Midwest, salt of the earth town, surrounded by a rural countryside. There was much to be done by men and women who lived by their hands. Not everyone wanted to leave the countryside to live out their lives in the newer town neighborhoods which were built after the war. It would remain to a future in which they would watch their children leave the town behind, when jobs, and wages, and benefits were no longer available there. And their parents did not want to live in the cities to which their children moved, when their sons and daughters left them alone in this small, decreasing town.

I was just a boy, Richard Blake's son, and I did not understand that Mr. Roberts was the kind of man for whom work and family was not all. Work and family were the only things for most of the families that lived in my neighborhood, on the surface of life that was visible to outsiders. None of the families in the surrounding neighborhoods belonged to his private country club, which was appropriately built on the highest hill in town. My mother did not have time to go to the club to sunbathe by its shimmering pool, nor to paint skillfully rendered copies of famous paintings on canvases using genuine artist oils for her own personal fulfillment. We did not go to Florida each winter, and unfortunately, we did not drive a convertible when the weather allowed, and a leather seated air-conditioned sedan when it did not. I did not even know if my parents were happy, no one ever talked about those things. Maybe some of the adults in my life were happy enough for no other reason except that they had survived the war, though two brothers in our family had not. Everyone knew someone who had been killed.

I never realized how limited we were and how disadvantaged our lives. I did not understand what it was to have wanderlust, and the ability to pay for it without guilt when you went to church on Sundays, and looked up at the men and women depicted in colors of glass.

I liked talking to the men out back in the warehouse, back by the conveyor tower that carried the sand and gravel which was loaded onto trucks. I was not allowed in a truck when it drove under the tower and was filled for a job. But I liked climbing into the trucks at other times and liked to help sweep out the back of a truck when it returned from a job if the driver let me help him. I liked being around these men and trucks as much as I liked being around my grandparents on the farm. They all worked with their hands and I did too when I was around them. There was an honest simplicity about the best of them. I learned later that this was not true about all of them, but that it was true of most of the people in any group of men or women, no matter how they made their living.

Mr. Roberts was frequently absent. He was a semi-professional race car driver who followed the circuit from track to track whenever he had the chance to drive. If he was away from the office in the summertime, I liked to ride my bicycle through town to the sand and gravel pit and take lunch to my dad. My mother fried hamburgers and toasted the buns on the frying pan. She wrapped them in aluminum foil so they stayed warm and the buns stayed crispy until I got to the office. I was allowed to get a soda from the machine the drivers used and then I pulled up a chair to the desk so that my dad and I could eat together.

All the trucks had radios in them. If a driver radioed the office, or my dad called one of them about a job, he used the microphone that sat on his desk. When you pressed a button on the base you could talk, and when you let it up, you could listen. I did not know anyone else who had to use such a device. You had to be pretty important to have a radio like that in your car, and you could always tell who had one by the long antenna attached to the trunk or bumper. Both the roadster and the convertible that Mr. Roberts drove had the long whip-like antennas on them. My dad's Ford did not.

Mr. Roberts was the most generous man I ever knew. He had Christmas parties each year for all of the employees and their families at his house. The gifts he gave to all the children were usually the best ones they received at Christmas. These were always my best Christmas gifts – an electric train, or the latest Fanner Fifty Cowboy Six-Shooter, complete with a leather holster. Mrs. Roberts talked to each of the parents so that she was able to buy the special gifts that all the children wanted. I was surprised that they were so good with children because they did not have a child of their own.

Each Christmas dinner was a feast, and many times something was served that I had never heard of, like the year it was a clam bake, and I could not believe that the clams were still alive when they were put into a steaming container of boiling water, so I had to see for myself, and they were. The children always wanted to go into the den, because Mr. Roberts had a cabinet full of shiny trophies and old racing helmets, and he let us try on the helmets and imagine that we were race car drivers, too. He was an adventurer and a risk taker, and over the years of racing he learned a lot about human nature, and the stress of a dangerous sport. He took good care of his employees, expecting an honest day's work, and giving good pay in return. He knew how to work with men, and he cared about their families.

It was a great shock to my father, the night the police chief came to the door. I was in bed, but heard the doorbell and the knock on the door, and voices from the living room below, and later the quiet murmur of voices from the kitchen where my mother and father sat talking, late into the night. Mrs. Roberts had asked the police chief to let my father know what happened, the only one outside of the family to be told, with a request that he come to see her in the morning. I know that there was not much sleep that night in our home, and that a grieving cry was also heard throughout the night at the other.

John Roberts died in a racing accident, when the car he was driving crashed into a retaining wall at the Indiana International Speedway.

In the morning there was not much more to tell. Richard Blake sat with the Roberts widow at her kitchen table over tea and the bitter truth. It was early, seven o'clock, because he would have to be at the plant before eight to open up and tell the men the news. In a few minutes my dad and John's wife would both be alone, he at the company, and his wife at home.

Roberts had enjoyed frequent adventures, and had left his wife much of the time on her own. Even when he was at home there was always business to attend to, and other business-related activities of the entrepreneur that he was. He was well respected in the business community. Over the years she had come to accept all of his outside activities, but he was a good provider and allowed her much independence both financial and personal, and she had the wherewithal to pursue her interests independently.

The business would be sold. Roberts had been a risk taker, and had died taking calculated risks during a NASCAR race. That was how he had run his business, other smaller business and investment interests, and lived his life. But he was also a prudent businessman in ways that would surprise some after his death. He had worked with a good lawyer, and what his lawyer had tried to convince him to do, he had done. There was never a question of succession for his company, it would not be his widow's burden to decide the fate of the company. It had already been decided in the event of his death.

Roberts had appointed a company that would begin the purchase and takeover of his Sand & Gravel Company in the event of his death. By the end of the day, the way was clear and the tasks were in motion. All of the late husband's affairs were to be put in order for the grieving widow. John's lawyer was now his widow's lawyer, and she would be taken good care of, too. All this was explained to Richard. John Roberts had arranged that he would have a job for life with the new company if he should choose to stay. Mrs. Roberts was happy that in this crisis Richard need not worry about his own security. He could continue to be the experienced office manager in charge of the business and provide stability for the new owners.

There was one last thing that the widow had to tell him, something that not just the lawyer, but also John's banker had been involved with. Mrs. Roberts bent her head to the table, and slowly and carefully told Richard what he needed to do for John on behalf of his last act of charity and need. Richard too, bent his head to meet hers at the table, and he listened silently. He inhaled deeply and let his breath out slowly, and then consented to do the one last thing.

Richard called his wife from the office at quitting time that day, when he was ready to close up the office and go home. He told her not to wait dinner. He had to help with some of the business affairs due to the death, the new ownership, and the widow. He closed the office at the usual time, and drove to the home of the new widow Roberts to receive an envelope, address, and the phone number. Then he drove to the edge of town by the high school football stadium and tennis courts to use the pay phone in the telephone booth there. He made a call and noted the directions, and on the piece of paper on which the phone number was written, he wrote down the directions, using the tiny desk of triangular aluminum in the corner of the booth underneath the telephone. The brief conversation to meet was over, and for a few moments he held the black Bakelite telephone receiver in his hand after withdrawing it from his left ear. In his right hand he still held the pen that he always carried in his shirt pocket. He wished that everything could have been taken care of with a phone call, but he knew that this was not possible.

It is surprising how steep the hills are south and west of the town. Most of the townspeople never took the roads here that went past the old, unused burial park, the old school, and the St Peter church that had been converted into a home after the war. That is why it is still called Apostle Church Road, though it is highly unlikely that any rock could be struck here by a prophet and bring forth water. What was struck was coal, and it was here that the strippers laid waste to the hills surrounding the town in the years between and after the wars. No one remembered why the road was named German Hill Road, especially since it wound its way south to the old canal towpath near an old French pioneer settlement. There was no reason to go into these hills if you did not live there, because there were easier ways to get from one side of the valley to another. It was quiet here now, the coal was long ago stripped out, and the big machines and the crews of coarse men were gone. You could live privately and quietly in these hills.

He found the house, and a young woman opened the door and he entered the front hall. In a few moments she would be the second woman to cry over the death of the well-known local businessman, whose race car had crashed into a racetrack wall. She thanked Mr. Blake for his visit and the envelope, took his hand, and embraced him as he offered her his condolence. Without entering further into the home, he turned and left. She would also be taken care of by the adventurer who had died, and who in death, was perhaps more tidy than in life.

10.
Bread Line Budapest

In the small state-run shops, there were always at least two full aisles of beer, wine, and liquor, but for a can of fruit or vegetables there was only one choice for each of the items you wanted to buy. The fresh meat and cheese counter, however, was usually well stocked, and if you knew how to ask for one pound, fél kiló, and the few words you needed for beef, ham, turkey, chicken, and cheese, and pointed at what you wanted to buy to clarify your strange accent, you could manage through the culture shock you felt here, in this ancient city that lay beyond the border, southeast of the frontier from Vienna. And you were delighted with the heavy, thick, and nutritious fresh bread which was always available in the shops, baked in huge state-run bakeries, sized only in standard one-kilo loaves. We did not live and shop where the diplomatic and state department families lived and shopped. We truly lived here, we lived on the economy. Those members of the military and employees of the State Department had the PX in which to shop for all the American brands, and this made all of the wives living and shopping on the still state-run economy, jealous.

There was only one grocery in our neighborhood, on the Pasaréti square at the bottom of the hill where we lived. If you had time, it was a treat to walk there for Sunday morning Mass at the Church of St Anthony of Padua. Flames surrounded the feet of my favorite saint, one of the painted images of fourteen saints, on the left wall facing the alter, below which we liked to sit. Pasaréti tér was a one kilometer walk from our home down a street which ended in sidewalk steps, and continued on paths lined by the fenced and gated gardens of the homes you passed along the way.

We were the only Americans in our neighborhood, and I never saw any others at the grocery, or at Mass at Páduai Szent Antal Plébánia, Saint Anthony of Padua Parish. The state shop and the Catholic church competed on opposite sides of the square. You had to shop every day or two, and the shop girls got to know you, and recognized your presence with a friendly nod. After a few weeks at Mass there was often a brown-robed brother or a parishioner who would come up to you to practice his English, or invite you for coffee, and ask why you were here in their country, which for so many years had been isolated from the west. The girls at the shop also knew that you bought premium cuts of choice meats in quantities that the average person did not often buy, but despite this they remained friendly if you were modest and friendly in return. They smiled at your language faux pas when you tried to speak their strange language, like the time my wife introduced me as her white man, instead of her husband, because the words for white and husband sounded similar, and it was the first time she tried to introduce me. Afterwards she never had to introduce me again.

Perhaps what the tired hotel manager once told me was true.

"Why do you want to live here?" he said to me when, after two months at the hotel on Margaret Island in the middle of the Danube, I checked my family out to move into a home in District II.

"Life is hard, it is not easy to live here," he sighed sympathetically, and shook his head as I signed the bill.

While there never seemed to be a shortage of choices for what you wanted to drink, finding what you wanted to eat was another matter, and here choices on the shelves for boxed and canned products were always limited. Certain foods were only available at special times of the year. Bananas and oranges were real treats, and until recently had only been available on holidays during the year. That would change after the wall came down and markets began to open up. But even after, it would be years before certain storage facilities were built, and before imported fruits and vegetables would be available year-round in fresh condition. Nitrogen storage was a technology not yet available here. By the time spring blossomed, and you bought potatoes at small sidewalk vegetable stands on the Pasaréti, your wife would cry at the amount of the rotted parts she would have to cut away before she cooked them. But fresh meat and cheese were always available. And now that the economy was liberalized, private businesses called Kfts began to open up everywhere, and at the end of the street on which we lived there was a small shop which stocked miscellaneous convenience items like milk, eggs, bread, beverages, and candy.

October of that first year brought new challenges to the nascent government and to life in this still great dowager city. The prime minister's health was a national concern, and a constant threat of financial insolvency weighed in the balance, much like the pressures that newly privatized companies faced as western joint ventures, and state enterprises struggled with currency valuations and inflationary pressures. The first Gulf War began when Iraq invaded Kuwait, and tensions increased in the east and west on both sides of the ocean. I had come here to work before the first free elections, and I would live here to attend the funeral procession on Andrássy út for József Antall three years later. He was the son of the aristocrat who had been arrested by the Gestapo in WWII, and who was himself arrested in 1956 while leading the Revolutionary Committee at the gymnasium school where he taught, and who forty years later would rise to become the first free prime minister.

During one week in the first fall of our residency, tensions rose as the government announced a large price increase for gasoline. The taxi drivers demonstrated against the threat to their livelihood, took to the streets and barricaded bridges. Roadways were blocked and movement in the country was increasingly paralyzed. Those of us with cars were able to cross the Danube to go to work with difficulty, but by Friday at the end of the first week of the strike, there were shortages in the food stores, and a growing concern that we would be unable to return to our homes at the end of the workday. The government decreed factories would continue to run where necessary; some critical workshops ran continuously day and night and could not be shut down, yet there was concern that essential utilities and energy sources could be rationed and disrupt our production. Offices in the city were closed, non-essential employees in factories were permitted to go home. We were told on which bridge it was still possible to cross the Danube, and which thoroughfares to avoid.

My secretary gave me the name of a bread factory still operating in a southern Buda district west of the river, because by the second week of the strike, the shelves in the food stores were empty except for beer and wine and spirits, as the people hoarded food supplies. We planned a trip to the factory, so that we could at least have bread over the weekend, with the balance of milk and eggs and juice which we still had on hand to feed our family. Restaurants would be open now only with difficulty, and the local eating places, éttermek, would either be filled to capacity or closed.

We decided to go together as a family to the bread factory. There would be one loaf per person available if you reached the factory early enough before they sold out their stock. My wife was navigator with the map, the children were in the back seat of my Lada Samara kocsi enjoying the adventure, while I nervously shifted the car into gear as we began our trip to the district south of where we lived.

We wound our way through the city following the curve of the Danube River from District II to District X without much difficulty. At the intersection of Hegyalja Street and Budaörsi Street, I waited for the traffic light to change and to cross over a huge cobblestone traffic circle. There was no way I could know that a military order had been given earlier in the day. Heavy equipment was now entering the capital in an attempt to control the six bridges spanning the Danube within the city limits. By now all major bridge crossings throughout the country were barricaded by the striking taxi drivers.

As I crossed the circle, I found my Lada passing much too close to a massive Russian tank trying to make the turn, sliding on the stones next to me. I sped up to get out of the way and exit the traffic circle, while this show of force headed towards the river and the bridges. I felt fear for the first time having heard the tank treads slapping and sliding against the cobblestones, and wondered for myself and for my family what it was that I was doing here, and why.

We continued on to the address of the factory that my secretary had given me and parked on the street as close to the entrance as possible. There were many cars here and a long line of customers had formed in front of a single small retail sales window that was positioned on the side of the building near the entrance. The window was still open and people were still buying bread so I queued up and waited my turn. We were all politely waiting to buy a single football shaped one-kilogram loaf of bread that the factory produced there. It was the standard bread that you could find in any shop, thick, heavy, nutritious, and delicious. My family waited in the car as I stood in line to make my purchase.

"One loaf please," I said to the uninterested worker behind the counter after I made my way to the front of the line.

"Egy kenyeret, kérem szépen," I said, trying to speak in my most polite Hungarian.

She handed me the loaf, a piece of paper covering her hand with which she gripped the crust as she handed it over to me. I gave her a few coins and paid for the bread.

"There is no doubt," I thought to myself as I turned to leave the sales window, "that I am the only foreigner here."

I returned to the car with my prize, and the three children filling the back seat insisted on taking turns to hold the still warm bread for the ride back to our home. Perhaps for the first time did I know, and finally understand, why it was that I was here.

11.
Ain't-ler Hills

It was a one stoplight country town. At the intersection was a filling station, grocery store, and a bank. Thirteen miles west lay the county seat, on the way over Route 31. The county seat was once a successful mid-western town surrounded by farmland and powered by agricultural products and services, and skilled labor shops. On Main Street before the war, you could find live theater, elaborate movie houses, and dance and supper clubs. The townspeople and the farmers from the surrounding fields walked the streets together on Saturday nights. It was home to an almost-famous celebrity who made his fame and fortune out west after the war. He traveled from the small stage of this farm country town to Hollywood. After the war, it really was hard to keep the boys who came home down on the farm.

If you wanted to do something on Saturday night, you drove the thirteen miles west to the county seat, because there was nothing to do in Antler Hills.

Driving east from the county seat on your return to quiet Antler Hills, you crossed the old iron bridge at the edge of town, the one that spanned the Lakosing River on Main Street, and then over Dry Wash before it turned to pastures that lined either side of Route 31. You would not recognize it today, because some of the farms that used to lay on either side of the road have been broken up, and here and there large homes have been built for the executives who survived the economic changes and replaced the farmers and trades people who once lived exclusively outside of the town proper. If you went back far enough in time, the early white settlers knew the Lakosing

River as Owl Creek, and the town existed because of the confluence of the river where grain mills, lumber mills, glass making, tanneries, general stores, and storehouses rose near its banks. These early townspeople would be happy to have seen the progress of the 19th and 20th centuries that followed after them. But if you went back even farther in time, it was the Indians of the Algonquin language who gave the river its name, Lakosing, the River of the Little Owls. These owls were the robin-sized Megascops asio, and they sang with a gentle neigh and soft warble. They lived among the forests which followed the river, whose waters eventually merged with other rivers to make its way from Midwestern hills to the Mississippi and the Gulf of Mexico. There are many things in the modern world that the Algonquins and other Native American tribes who spoke related languages admired. No doubt they would drop certain of their own cultural possessions to acquire some of these of the modern world – the most prized of all a gun with a rifled barrel. But they would no longer recognize the land and how it was transformed in the two hundred years after the arrival of the first white settlers who came to conquer it, not trade with it, as the French had done before them.

It is difficult to travel down these old country roads and not think of the past, and halfway between the county seat and Antler Hills you cross the Baltimore & Ohio railroad tracks, and then more farms which spread out from either side of the road all the way to Antler Hills. Or Ain't-ler Hills, as Milton liked to pronounce it. "AIN'T-LER" Hills he would repeat with emphasis and a thinly veiled contempt, perhaps because that is where he found himself, bitterly, in a one stoplight town. A guttural-pronunciation as unfriendly as his rightful demeanor.

A one stoplight midwestern country town in those days still had its own town marshal and deputy. And though it was a full-time job for the two officers who shared the duty with one patrol car, there was usually time for other activities as well, since a country town whose population never exceeded three thousand people was not a hotbed of criminal activity. Both the marshal and his deputy knew everyone in town, and everyone knew them as well. Alcohol was still the drug of choice long after the first settlers had arrived, and there was lots of drinking and drunk driving, too. But people were more forgiving back then, and you knew which cars and trucks and drivers you had to be careful about, and it was not always the men who did the drinking. Decent people were generally not on the roads late at night anyway. The occasional inebriate who ran off the road into a tree, or into a ditch, or drove off into an empty field when he did not negotiate a curve in the road, was managed with a small town's sympathy. There was rarely a serious injury, and more often than not, the driver walked home along the road or across a field, and retrieved the damaged vehicle in the morning, or as soon as the hangover permitted.

Sometimes the marshal or the deputy gave the remorseful driver a ride home, whose waiting wife or husband might prove to be a bit more unsympathetic than the law.

Earl was the town marshal, and he lived on a small farm with his wife who was also the town's dispatcher. JW was the deputy who also worked with his father at the body shop beside the trailer in which his mom and dad lived. Everybody knew everyone else, and there was enough pity to go around to those folks who had troubles without a meanness about them. Human weakness was more tolerated then than now, it was more personal and less judgmental. Later, when the farms were broken up or taken over by the corporations, and the mills closed and the shops moved overseas, drugs appeared, things changed, and life became harder. The county eventually assumed control of policing, and though the population gradually decreased, everyone no longer knew everyone else. There were more renters, not owners, and a more transient, more hurried, less secure, and a less familial population gave rise to a more impersonal town. Illegals seemed to arrive everywhere, though they were hardworking, quiet, and honest people. There was increased drug usage by the young people of the families that stayed, and the oil and gas people who came looking for jobs, as long as there was something to suck out of the ground before they moved on to the next drilling site.

The town marshal and his deputy worked twelve-hour shifts, seven days a week. There was no real time off. Half of all the hours you lived you were on call or on patrol, though it was a small town with a limited area to protect. There was always time for a break, or to do a chore at your farm, or to help at the body shop, or to have a coffee or a soda at Michie's Place on Main Street, or to get a haircut at the two-chair barbershop and catch up on the latest gossip. But you also had to put your badge on your uniform and go back on duty during your own time off if there was a problem and Earl's wife, Mabel, the dispatcher, called you and said you were needed. This could happen at any hour of the day. To be a marshal or deputy in a small town like that was a way of life, you were part of the fabric of the town, and you knew everyone by their first name. It might take three or four weeks to arrange for a day off, with double duty for the marshal or deputy who had to pick up the slack, and work your shift while you were away.

After the bank robbery, JW decided he needed a little bit of personal protection. There was a company in the state capital an hour's drive away that made a fiberglass bullet proof vest. It happened one day in the county seat, and a thirteen-mile run down the state highway. During the bank robbery a teller was killed. The getaway car came up the highway towards Antler Hills, chased by a police car which could not match its speed. Mabel received the call. JW was on duty and he blocked the road with his cruiser at the iron bridge that went into town across the North Fork River. When the bank robbers saw the roadblock and tried to cross the bridge, JW put three twelve-gauge deer slugs into the engine block and it come to a screeching halt. When the driver got out of the car with a gun in his hand, JW took part of that hand off with the fourth slug he fired. When he saw what happened to his partner, the other robber came out of the car with his hands over his head. The officer from the county seat where the bank robbery and killing took place finally caught up to the getaway car, but by then the four slugs fired by JW had ended it. The first three slugs went through the radiator, right in through the timing cover, busted the timing cam, shrapneled the butterfly as the slugs passed through the carburetor, shredded the fuel line, and started the car on fire. The fire department came in with sirens to put out the fire, and bandage up what was left of the first bank robber's right hand.

The patrol car from the county seat had not been able to keep up with the bank robber's Chevrolet. That car was faster than the patrol car that chased it from the scene of the crime. JW said later to a reporter that he had heard the engine of the getaway car coming down the road before he could see it approaching the bridge. He said he knew it was a fast car from the beautiful sound of the engine. He knew that it was a powerful, small-block Chevy V8, and he knew that the county cruisers were just not able to match its speed.

That incident was the highlight of JW's law enforcement career. Yellowing copies of the local paper's reporting of the event could be seen for years on the wall of the barber shop, behind the bar of Michie's soda fountain, and behind the counter of the local hardware and farm supply store. It was the only time JW ever got his picture in the paper. It was a front-page story, and in the picture, he was holding the police shotgun in both hands. Two smaller pictures featured what was left of the robber's bloody right hand, and the getaway car on fire.

It was after that shoot-out on the bridge that JW decided he needed the bullet proof vest. The vest company made a cast of his chest, and he chose an egg shell design that strapped the front and back sides together. It extended down only to his belt buckle so that he could sit comfortably for hours in the patrol car. It was made of twelve layers of imbedded fiberglass and in the middle, there was a layer of wire mesh. The vest was almost three quarters of an inch thick. The company claimed that it would stop a .38 caliber slug. When JW picked it up, they had him try it on, and then test fired a .38 special at a sample vest to show him its capability. It did stop the slug. And though any of the modern military style guns used today would have rendered the vest useless, JW said the .38 caliber bullet hardly made a dent in the thing, but it did knock it back pretty good.

Late one night, JW got a dispatch call from Mabel about a complaint called in on Milton. Milton had been working a lot of overtime. JW said that he and his wife Heddy were a fightin' and a feudin' over the extra money when he arrived at their home. Milton worked in one of the local shops. Heddy was a home maker. He wanted to spend the money on a used deer gun his buddy was selling. She thought it would be a good idea to stock up on some groceries because it was coming up on cold weather. Mabel told JW they had gotten into a real knock-down drag-out fight according to a close neighbor, who could hear the goings on at their house.

When Milton tried to use the phone to call his buddy about the deer gun, Heddy grabbed it off the wall and threw it in his direction. It took him right across the forehead with it. JW had known both Milton and Heddy his whole life. They were all kids together. When he got there, Milton was bleeding profusely from a deep cut on the superciliary arch above his left eye.

"Are you all happy now?" JW said to Heddy when she opened the front door for him.

She glared at him and did not answer. He went into the kitchen. There was blood all over the floor.

"Get me an ambulance!" cried Milton.

"Ambulance is on the way," replied JW, calmly.

"Your neighbors called Mabel, and said there was one big fight on here," JW said to both Milton and Heddy.

"They could see Milton's bloody face through the window, and Mabel called for an ambulance."

JW sat Milton down on a chair, while Heddy stood by the kitchen sink. He grabbed a paper towel from the counter and pressed it against Milton's head.

"Heddy, get me another paper towel," JW said.

"What for? Let him bleed!"

"Now would you please get me another towel?" JW repeated with authority, and she threw the whole roll at the deputy.

He put another towel up against Milton's bleeding head.

"Push on this as hard as you can until the ambulance arrives."

The phone had almost missed Milton's head. It only caught him by about half an inch. But the edge of the phone hit him at just the right place to cause a lot of bleeding, and would eventually require twelve stitches.

"Now Heddy, just settle down," JW said.

"I'm perfectly fine."

"That's good, ok, let me take care of hubby here," JW said, and turned back around to face her.

"But now Heddy, you know you did wrong."

"Really?" she screamed.

With that she picked up a kitchen knife off the counter, and pffttt, she threw it at the deputy, and it stuck into the new bullet proof vest which covered his chest, that she did not know was underneath his shirt.

She immediately turned white when she saw what she had done, fainted, and slumped to the floor. She now lay at the foot of her husband, who was still sitting in a chair at the kitchen table, bleeding from the cut above his eye.

The ambulance arrived and the EMTs rushed in. Milton was bleeding badly, Heddy was on the floor, and JW was bent over both of them, with the knife still sticking out of the bullet-proof vest which covered his chest.

"JW, what is going on here?" the EMTs asked, incredulous at the scene.

"Don't worry about me or her," JW said and he pulled the knife from his vest.

They crossed the floor to Milton who let out a loud yell as they pressed the wound to staunch the bleeding, and then put butterfly type bandages on to hold the wound closed. Stitches would come later. The EMTs glanced at the deputy as he laid the kitchen knife back on the counter.

Heddy started to come to, and JW helped her up.

"Now, are you all right?" he inquired.

"Yea, yea," she mumbled, "yea, yea. Yes, I think I'm OK now."

"Now you know I have to take that knife as evidence. You and I are going to have to go before the judge on this."

"Yea, yea, OK," she said, "yes, OK, OK."

Milton blew his top. "What do you mean you are taking her to the judge? I'm the one that's hurt!"

The ambulance EMTs just shook their heads as they got up to leave, and JW turned to them.

"I've known these people since I was born, everything is under control."

The deputy sat both husband and wife at the table.

"First thing is, I'm not going to arrest anyone, because you would have to spend the night in jail, and then you'd have to go before the judge in the morning. I'd have to do all the paperwork and I don't want to do it tonight. Will you two promise me to come before the judge at ten o'clock tomorrow morning?"

He waited as they both looked at one another.

"Now do you promise, both of you to be there?"

"Oh yea. Yea. Yes," they both replied.

Milton was in pretty bad shape, the left eye was already black and blue and closing, and Heddy sat quietly beside him, shaken. JW, tired after another long day, left them alone and went home.

The next morning in court, the Judge admonished Heddy while her husband sat silently beside her. The local hospital emergency room had just stitched up his forehead.

"Heddy, you are just not supposed to do what you did to your husband."

The Judge shook his head, nodded at Milton's black and blue face, and picked up the knife and looked at it.

"And then you know, you threw this knife, and stuck it into JW,' he continued.

"Yes, sir, I did," she admitted, "I'm afraid I did."

"What do you plead?"

"I'm guilty as all get out, JW is my friend, and I'm not going to go any other way."

"OK, in that case, here is what we are going to do. JW says he wants leniency for both of you, because he's known you all his life."

"I'm going to charge you ten dollars for court costs," he said, raising his voice, "and I don't want to see either of you in here again!"

"Case Dismissed!"

It had all come down to money in this one stoplight country town, Antler Hills, where there was not that much to do, and everyone knew everyone else.

"Well, Judas Priest, there's no place like AIN'T-LER Hills," Milton liked to sneer, whenever he talked and complained about this or that, with a scowl on his face.

Milton wanted to spend the money on this, and Heddy wanted to spend the money on that. And truthfully, in those times, groceries would have been the much better choice, than the used deer rifle that Milton wanted to buy.

12.
A Sunday Dinner and 1956

Székely Tamás sat at the head of the long wooden table Sunday evening in a restaurant on the village square. The restaurant was opened for Tamás by the owner whom he knew. It was opened for him alone, because all the restaurants were always closed on Sundays, as were all the shops and stores. He needed to find a restaurant for the travelers from the capital who arrived on Sunday so they could start their meetings early Monday morning. There was no time to waste. The due diligence was finished long ago, and the takeover was complete. Now there was much work to do, and the foreign management team was still being put into place to take control of the largest enterprise in the country.

As long as Tamás could remember, no one had ever arrived on a Sunday for a meeting scheduled to begin on Monday morning, and there was no understanding the inconvenience this caused, nor was there any care about it. Actually, this was not true. We did know that traveling with a team on a Sunday was something new and inconvenient. It was a statement of change and an exercise of authority, an expression about the condition of the business, and the urgency in which we had found ourselves. But there were many things that were not understood that would become inconvenient, many justified, some unjustified, or just plain misunderstood, by the members of the new team of foreigners. It was all part of the work required if the first major joint venture behind the former iron curtain was to be successful. All of the managers in the factory would be involved in the meetings, and by the end of the week it was expected that there would be a basic understanding of the factory's production and financial structure.

The drive across the countryside had been pleasant enough, but much too hot and uncomfortably stuffy in the small box Lada, whose motor strained at speed with the full cargo of four men, and one woman. Beyond the boundaries of the capital there were no four lane highways, and we soon found ourselves on a two-lane road heading west. To control the noise and the battering of the wind at highway speed, with all five seats occupied and no air conditioning, the windows remained closed. There were no rest stops along the way, but we made use of the high grasses that lined parts of the highway for nature stops during our three-hour journey. First stop was for the woman to squat in the tall grass, after the driver moved the car modestly forward on the shoulder of the road. When she returned to the car, the men got out with their backs to the road, to stand and do their business. The spring fields were plowed, and there were still teams of horses that worked in smaller fields, but all of the enormous state-run fields that ran to the horizon were now tended by tractors. Though not on this Sunday afternoon. When the car was pulled over and the engine turned off, there were no sounds, just a gentle breeze and the susurrus of the grasses lining the field, like the sound of a woman's Hungarian peasant dress in the motion of a dance.

Tamás was small of stature but big of heart. He had a girth large for his size, and wore glasses that framed and made his eyes look large and luminous. He moved and spoke with an intensity of enthusiasm and emotion, in constant motion, energetically bringing all around the table, making sure glasses were filled with the locally brewed beer and barreled wine. He welcomed the American and the few colleagues from headquarters with the formal graciousness and confidence of an ancient, proud, cultured tradition. The American, the guests from headquarters, and his factory managers were brought together to the table.

But before we proceeded with business, he began to tell us, including the foreigner among us whom he had met for the first time that afternoon, here in his own town, far from the company headquarters, the true story of his life. Tamás sat at the head of the table, the American sitting opposite at the other end, the factory managers and headquarters colleagues seated on either side between them.

Tamás rose from his seat.

"Székely Tamás, a nevem. My name is Tamás Székely."

"Én vagyok itt a gyárigazgató. I am the factory manager here. I have worked for this company for thirty-four years, ever since I became an apprenticed machine mechanic at the age of seventeen, in 1956."

"A machine mechanic is a highly skilled worker, and our factory depends on the mechanical skills of these men in order to produce the products that we make in our factory, on the machines for which they are responsible to operate and to maintain. I am proud to have started on the factory floor, to have been taught and educated by the men who learned the job, and acquired the skills before me. These jobs are the highest skilled and highest paid positions in our factory, but this is not the work that I intended to do when I was seventeen years of age."

With that introduction, and just after having met this man a few minutes before, he opened his suit coat and raised his shirt above his belt to expose his body. Holding his clothes up in his left hand, he pointed with his right hand to a scar that began at the front of his chest above and to the right side of his stomach. Turning around, he pointed to another larger scar that continued on the same side of his body on his lower back.

"This is why I am now a factory manager, and not the professor of history that I wished to become when I graduated from gymnasium."

He lowered his shirt and suit coat to cover his body and continued, still standing formally at the head of the table. Now his eyes moistened with the distilled memory of decades past, his voice strongly projecting and filled with liquid emotion.

"October 1956," he began. He paused, looking down to see back through time, and then returned his gaze to those assembled at table.

"It was the first time that we expected the Americans would come. Now, thirty-four years later you are here, and we welcome you at last, and we are glad for your help, and for your knowledge, and for your support as we ready ourselves, our business, and our country for a new future. Later, in the next month of this new spring, there will be for me the first free election of my life in which I will be able to participate."

His moistened eyes filled, tears flowed down his face and stained his glasses in an open display of emotion to the American he had met only a few minutes before, as we sat down together to the Sunday evening table.

"I was just a young student, accepted to university in the capital city, and I planned for an academic career. I had excellent grades and a good intellect, many friends, and life was good in our city. The many cafés were the places in which we met and debated. We were very young, and suddenly we found ourselves swept up in the emotion and promise of throwing off the oppression we believed we could overthrow, because we were very young. We felt possibility and hope in the optimism of youth. The demonstrations seemed to happen spontaneously, almost despite ourselves, and we were swept up."

"I was one of the first students shot."

"On October 23 we gathered at the base of the Buda Castle Funicular, ready to cross the Danube on the Bridge of Chains. We assembled at the Parliament on the other side of the river to join thousands of other protesters already gathered there. I found myself in the crowd outside Radio Budapest. From the programs on Radio Free Europe, we believed that the west, especially the Americans, were going to come to our aid. We announced this hope with loudspeakers on the streets. We naively thought we could enter the radio building and broadcast our demands of freedom, which we believed would be taken up by the citizens of Budapest, by America, and by the citizens of the world to throw off the oppression that we so naively believed was our right to overthrow."

Tamás paused and took off his glasses, dried and polished the lenses with a cloth. He looked down, past the years as he did this, his eyes focused on something we could not see, his mind turning back through to the time when he was young. He replaced his glasses on his nose and put the cloth away, straightened his shirt and his coat, looked up, swallowed, and forced a smile with his mouth closed, and again he addressed the table. As he returned again to the present, there was not a sound in the room from the table of listeners.

"The radio building was protected by the Államvédelmi Hatóság, the AVH, the State Security Force. Although some Hungarian soldiers took our side against the AVH, we were fired upon. Some died, and I was shot through from front to back. Somehow, I survived and was hidden with the help of friends. I could not go to hospital for fear of arrest and perhaps execution, and I could no longer attend my classes. My dreams of an academic life were over, and I would not be permitted to attend university again."

"With one shot fired by the AVH from the radio building on that first day, October 23, the revolution was over for me. By the time I completed my convalescence, the revolution was over for all of us who had gathered that day outside the Parliament and Radio Budapest, on Kossuth Lajos tér. But I was one of the lucky ones and have lived to see today, thirty-four years later, this day at last."

"We were bitterly disappointed with the Americans. We felt betrayed and abandoned by the West. We would never again trust completely in Radio Free Europe. But finally, now, after these so many years, you have come. I am no longer young, but

I welcome you with the hope that my optimism can be as innocent and fulfilled as that of a young man, so many years before in 1956."

There was silence in the room. After a few moments all eyes again were dry. Most at the table were too young to have experienced the failed revolution, only one or two at table were present in that city long ago, though all knew the history of that day, and the months and years to follow. Of those seated here, only Tamás had participated directly in the activities now celebrated as a national holiday each year on October 23, the anniversary of his long-ago protest and injury. At long last his story, and his bitterness, were expatiated and freed.

The former machine mechanic sat down, now a proud factory manager of the largest enterprise in his country. He laughed to himself, paused to think for a moment, then stood again with his head held high, and raised his glass in a simple toast to the future, with all gathered around the table.

"To our health, az egészségünkre!"

13.
The Barber and The Old Man

Kaleigh asked me if I believed in God, and before I could answer her question, she said she believed in Jesus and Heaven and Hell. She moved to the other side and cut a little more and it fell to the floor like the cottony seeds that float and fill the air in late spring. I did not want to disappoint her and I told her that I wasn't sure.

"There are many things we do not understand. But I surely believe that we make our own heaven or hell right here on earth. Perhaps one day we will all understand."

She had come to the house, extending her lunch hour to cut the old man's hair at his home. He used to go into town to her barbershop, and though he was almost ninety-five years old, he still had a full head of hair, and with the mane of his untrimmed beard and hair that now reached to his shoulders, he looked like a Russian author or a civil war general. His clean shirt was soiled only where he wiped his mouth on the sleeve, and his faded jeans were torn, though they had just been laundered. He was still strong enough to go to town, but the old man did not want to be embarrassed by his appearance if he went to the barber now, and I did not want to have to explain how he still was able to live alone to any of the curious men waiting to have their turn in the chair, each of them young enough to be his son, his grandson, or even his great-grandson. He looked like a modern-day hermit, but it was only through a lack of effort or fatigue. He did not live apart from the rest of the town. It was simply the fact that in the months after he no longer drove his car, he had begun to let his hair and beard grow. And he had also begun to let himself go.

Five years earlier, Kaleigh's brother died. He was not yet thirty. But still every day Kaleigh talked about Jesus and Heaven and Hell and the brother who had died. The day before he died, she said she heard a voice in her right ear while she was driving home from work, and the voice told her that she should go back to see her brother. But she had been so busy that day, and besides, she had just left him after a full day at the shop where he cut hair in the chair next to hers. By the next morning he was dead. It took several months before the coroner's report came. It hurt her to finally know after months of grief that her brother had suffered from a massively enlarged heart. He was a gentle giant of a man who had worked beside her for almost ten years in the shop below the ballroom dance hall on Main Street Square. He was not supposed to die so young. She said she would always regret not listening to the voice, and not going back to the shop to see her brother one more time before he died.

She parked on the street in front the house, came up the concrete steps where the morning glory vines swirled around the lamp post set beside the last step. She walked up to and ascended the wooden steps to the porch, its columns beginning to sag with the weight of the old roof and all the years in which the old man had lived there. She crossed the porch as I opened the front door, and she came in.

All of her things were packed into the small suitcase she brought with her, and she unfolded it open on the floor beside the kitchen table. The old man came into the room with a quiet hello and seated himself on a stool between the kitchen table and the kitchen sink, let her wrap him in the barber's cape, and she began to work on him, first the hair, and then the beard.

A few years after her brother's death her father had a heart attack and died, she said. He was unconscious with no pulse for several minutes before the EMS arrived at their home and he was declared dead, but when he reached the hospital, he was revived and he lived. Her father told Kaleigh that he had been with his mother, with her brother, and with other dead relatives. He asked his son if he could see the pearly gates, but her brother told him no, he had to go back because it was not his time. Her father did survive, woke up in intensive care, and regretted the waking up because he had wanted to stay in heaven to be with his mother and with his son. It frightened his wife to think that he wanted to stay in heaven and leave her alone on earth. Kaleigh understood her mother's fear, but she was happy because she believed in Jesus and Heaven and Hell, and she knew that her father had been in Heaven for a little while, and was with her brother who was already there. Although her father had been torn between the living and the dead, it comforted her to know that he had seen the better place, that her brother was safe, and that she had heard his greetings from Heaven.

The old man said nothing as I watched her cut his hair, while she talked to me about Jesus and Heaven and Hell, and her brother, her father, and her mother. He had seen enough of Hell when he had to dive into foxholes in the South Pacific, bombed and strafed by the people who now designed and built the Japanese car he drove. He had made his peace long ago, but he still remembered the A20's exploding on the tarmac, or falling into the sea, and of all the men whom they had lost and left behind in WWII. Still, he didn't want to talk about Jesus or Heaven either, and he was through with Hell. There was no point, he would tell me later, before he died.

"I try to hold down the worries," he said to me one day, when I asked him what kinds of things he thought about.

"There's no point to it."

"I'm OK."

14.
The Double Standard Bra

Hope wasn't like the other women I'd known. Oh sure, she was slim with great hips, legs you wanted to squeeze till your hands fell off, a profile that, well, you just had to see it when she crossed her legs and sat on the stool in my kitchen, and then that mouth that invited kisses that blinded me on the edge of a cliff without a safety rope to stop me from falling down. In other words, she was perfect.

She made me crazy, as if I wasn't crazy enough to begin with. At least I thought so.

Maybe I should have known better. After all it had taken a while before she even agreed to take her shoes off in front of me. I loved her size, but she wisely did not even trust me with her shoes. I'd suggest she get comfortable by slipping them off, but she said she'd heard all those lines before and let me know in no uncertain terms.

"I'm on to you, Mister," she would say.

Then she would toss me off the cliff.

So, if I had that much trouble trying to find my way to uncover her tiny feet, you can imagine the trouble I had with those spaghetti straps on her bra, especially when she immediately sat up, came to attention, and tried to intimidate me.

She would coyly say, "What are you doing?"

As if she didn't know exactly what I was doing, why I was doing it, and what I really wanted to do with it, each time I came close to that paradise which lay beneath one of her impregnable spaghetti strap bras.

I explored the sweetness of her mouth with my tongue, and her hands slipped under my shirt. I pulled her on top of me and she began to kiss my chest.

"Please, please, please let me kiss you, too," I pleaded.

I tried to sit up to embrace her, my hands began to search her body.

"It's not fair."

But she pushed me back down onto the cushions with both hands.

"It doesn't have to be fair," she whispered as she bit my ear, then kissed it with her tongue.

"It's a double standard."

15.
Crescent Beach

After an afternoon at the beach, we were all back at the apartment. The children were washed and dressed, and the sea shells they collected were put out in the lanai to dry. I asked Stefania if she wanted to look for sand dollars on the way back along the beach to her place. This was her first time at the Gulf coast, and she helped my wife and I bring the children up from the beach that day and bring them back to our apartment, just arrived after her flight from Milan. I collected her from the airport earlier in the day, and brought her straight to the beach in order to spend the afternoon with us and visit for a few days.

Three years earlier she taught our son to play the violin, helping him to scratch out the scales and melodies of a beginner. She was a student at the Zeneakadémia, The Franz Liszt Academy of Music in Budapest, one of a group of musician friends with whom we shared our life. Stefania volunteered to find a violin for our son and to became his teacher. It was now more than a year since we left our life there, and returned to the States to live.

I agreed to meet Stefania at the Zeneakadémia. It was a short walk to Andrássy Street, and from there we took a tram to the old violin shop on Sziv utca. The decades-old tram bumped and rattled on its way from Vörösmarty utca to Sziv utca, its iron wheels screeching on the rails, and casting sparks from the overhead trolley pole. Stefania and I held onto the leather straps hanging above us, aside one another in the swaying, crowded, overheated car.

We arrived to an ancient looking shop, blackened with age on the outside, but whose interior was lighted and colored by the rich, wooden, brown and red hues of stringed instruments and paneled walls. There were instruments of all sizes, shapes, and conditions, from concert instruments to the ones that we had come for, a 3/4 sized violin for a beginning student. Stefania spoke with one of the luthiers, and she played several instruments, picking out the best one for the size and sound and a modest price. A case was brought out, but the tuning pegs were too wide, and the head of the violin did not fit into the case. A crude adjustment was made too quickly, I thought, and later when I arrived home with the violin, the pegs would not tighten properly to hold the strings in tune. It would require an adjustment to the holes in the pegbox, so that the tuning pegs would insert far enough and hold the strings taut.

After the purchase we both returned to the Zeneakadémia, where Stefania continued her practice session, and I retrieved my car to drive to Villányi út in District 11 in order to rescue my other son from a piano lesson in the Bösendorfer room of his teacher's flat, not the Steinway room this week, where he normally took his lesson.

His lessons took place in an elegant old building, with marble steps and ornately carved balustrades and decorative wrought iron railings. The large pre-war apartments in this building had been taken over by the state after the war, and subdivided into awkwardly sized flats. Nothing had been maintained or changed since the war ended, and the flats were complete with leaking pipes, ancient fixtures, and ill-fitting doors and windows. But you could still perceive with a certain amount of regret, the former elegance and privileged life which once took place there.

Stefania and I talked about all of these things, as we left to walk along the beach on the way to her apartment which sat directly on the sand beside the water. A storm the night before left a gouge in the beach from the dunes all the way to the water's edge, and I lifted her up into my arms so that she would not have to take off her tennis shoes and walk through the water. I could feel the warmth of her body like a child as I lifted her across, the same way I had carried my children, one after another, in this fashion.

We walked to the water's edge and spread our towels on the sand. Another storm would come later in the night, and the wind was beginning to blow gently seaward as the tide began to go out. Other bathers were already leaving the beach. They would all return later to watch the sunset over the Gulf. We entered the water, walking then swimming till the water covered our shoulders as we stood, and we began to feel for the sand dollars with our feet, far enough from the water's edge so that the shells were not already picked over. Each time we gently felt a sand dollar with our feet, Stefania dove beneath the water's surface until her legs disappeared, and she reached for the shells on the bottom. As we gathered up our seashells, we put them on our float to carry them back to the beach.

She delighted in the shelling and the gentle patterns on the tops of the sand dollars she brought to the surface, drops of water running down her face and dripping from her hair as she placed the treasures on the float.

Once, during a Christmas together in Italy, we met her father in front of the Duomo. There was a Milanese warmth between them, a quiet grief never repaired after the loss of her mother, his wife. It pleased her to show us the great cathedral, and its rooftop, like a city square in the sky. Then a walk down the Via Santa Margherita, past La Scala and a poster for an opera conducted by Ricardo Muti. We walked along the Via Meravigli and the Corso Magenta to the convent Santa Maria delle Grazie, and Da Vinci's great masterpiece on the deteriorating convent wall, feeling transfixed between a fading world of the past and the present. Now all of that too, here at the beach, was past.

The wind began to pick up, and it pushed our float against us, away from the beach. It was time to go in, and though the water was still warm, the air had become cooler. The tide and the wind made it difficult to swim against the outgoing water, pushing us out and away from shore, and we noticed now that we were the only ones still in the water. We could not let ourselves be pushed out further into the Gulf. We laughed, held onto the float, and paddled with our legs until we overcame the wind and the tide and moved toward the beach until we could stand and walk onto the sand.

For a few moments in the water, we had been afraid, and we laughed about it as we walked to her place on the beach. Then I continued on along the sand to my waiting family.

It is now many years past, and from this same beach a gulf has widened against time, much in life has changed, as far away now as the waters flow to a distant shore. In the brief moments between the memory of Stefania and the present time, there still remains an ancient city and luthier shop, music heard on the street from the open windows of a music academy, a lost mother and a gentle father, and a fading masterpiece on the plastered wall of an ancient convent. Finally, a last remembrance of the shells which we collected, and then a swim against the tide to bring them back to the beach.

16.
Remember Me

The fields of the swamp farms south of the city are black with fertile soil. They exude a pungent smell of decaying life and the promise of fertility, and extend from the river to meet the hills. Cara carefully parked her car beside one of the fields of muddy, black, plowed rows. In the distance she could see the lights from the cars on the road reflected off the surface of flowing water. But these were on the other side of the river. On this side of the river, it was dark. But it was still too bright to see the band of the Milky Way, hidden by the distant lights of the city which illuminated the evening sky like a halo. She felt at peace as she left the car, and the night descended upon the fields by the river, and she felt it descend upon her also, a calming final presence in the midst of the fecundity of nature.

A few years earlier and a lifetime ago, she came to my house on Rügy utca, and was very happy to be with all of the other girls. I came down the steps to greet the group of seven and asked her why, though, she had not taken the train to Prague, and it embarrassed her when she told me that she had not been invited. She was the gentlest of the girls, and the most-shy until you began to talk to her, then you could see the common sense she had, and the need and the wanting to communicate. She was not unattractive, but she was not the kind of girl you would look at twice in passing, not like some of the others who always tried to dress with more style. You can always tell when a woman is used to the attention of men. The attention that Cara had known was quite different.

All the other girls that stood in the group on the street outside my home were director's wives, but Cara's husband was not a director. He was at a level below and worked for one of the other directors, whose wife now stood beside her. That kind of social ranking affects the way you are able to behave when you are within an expatriate community in a foreign country. It simply had not occurred to any of the other wives to invite Cara to that trip to Prague, and if they had invited her, there were certain subjects they would not have been able to discuss. It all made perfect sense. None of it was mean spirited, or meant to be exclusionary, and because of that none of it really made any sense, as is so often the case with events that are the result of omissions or commissions, innocently though thoughtlessly made.

The overnight train to Czechoslovakia was a ten-hour adventure for the girls. There was always a story to tell about something that happened in the sleeping cars with two, four, or six bunks to a compartment. For this particular trip it was six and no room for a seventh. Even though compartment doors were latched, and valuables were safely tucked beneath pajamas and even within underclothing, gossip had it that thefts still occurred. There were rumors of sleeping gas and thieves who entered compartments silently without detection and were able to steal someone's valuables in the most titillating ways. It was to be an adventure anticipated like a game of hide and seek, planned beforehand and recounted afterwards with excitement at the embassy club. That day in front of my house with Cara, two of the girls were still speaking about an intimate theft that had occurred on the train during their adventure. I had come outside to say hello. That was when Cara cheerfully told me that she had lost nothing since she had not been on the train.

In the beginning, none of the men could help but notice the young working women in one way or another, when we arrived so soon after the Wall fell. Unmarried young women wore their natural beauty openly, the more revealing the clothing, the less likely the girl was married. Both men and women seemed to age quickly once they married and had families. Wealthy foreigners held power in the eyes of young women who could barely afford undergarments, or who chose not to wear them. If you worked late in the office, you might share a lift between floors with one of the night shift young women who cleaned the offices on a daily basis. If they entered the small lift with you, they might have trouble managing a vacuum, attachments, and a bucket in their hands, while trying to keep the buttons on the front of their thin threadbare work shifts closed. The fabric was so thin and flimsy it sometimes opened up and let their bodies spill out. They wore the simple, universal, inexpensive uniform of these low paid and vulnerable workers, through which you could see whatever it was that they could afford to wear or not to wear underneath.

Openness was natural and was taken for granted by the people in both the city and the countryside. Almost all had only modest possessions. Behavior was natural and human among people. The nature of this sort was accepted, along with unisex changing rooms and public nudity. These were things that jarred the sensibilities of new expatriates, who were not as sophisticated as the foreign posted state department officials or their European colleagues.

That was the cause of the trouble that Cara's husband got himself into when he took advantage of, and did not understand and abide by, the culture of physical openness. Working late in a factory which had been taken over by his western joint venture, he began a relationship with a young custodial worker, a beautiful young village girl who was without higher education. None could blame her if she took a chance and allowed herself to be taken advantage of, and to take her own advantage.

Each night when she entered his office to clean the room, Cara's husband had begun to notice the size and shape of the young woman's body. He measured her shape beneath the loose working clothes and compared it to that of his wife who was still young but twenty years older. Physical beauty was something you could see and enjoy at the public pools or the mineral baths, a public nudity taken for granted. It was not unusual or immodest behavior. But Cara's husband did not understand this. He did not understand that this was the cultural norm to be enjoyed as a small celebration of life and beauty which cost nothing to those who had little.

Cara's husband began to think that he could have this young woman. He brought small gifts to her and she began to seek his attention during her shift for a few minutes of escape. Soon her world would expand and his would become more difficult. She became pregnant with a child she said was his, at the same time that there was no child by choice in the marriage to his wife.

You could not argue that the foreigners were tempted and taken advantage of. It was easy to mistake a willing attentiveness as something personal, when it was nothing more than a fear for the future and unknown changes which were about to come. There was a need to perform for, and serve the new foreign leaders. There was a need to show that you were worthy in this new commercial world. It was a chance to bet on the future and to benefit from the chance.

Later, back home, the fields are where in my mind I still imagine her. I remember the fields and farms of my own small town, and the farmer's market at the edge of town. I imagine Cara, and the comfort that memories like this might have brought to her. The smell of the earth and the fields, of strawberries and the sweet smell of orchards, and of newly mown hay. The earthy smell of a plowed field. But by then it was too late for her, and the comfort became a grieving regret. Life became a symbol of emptiness after the harvest. This was long after. It was much before that the seeds of the story were planted.

Growing up they were a happy family. Cara was an only child whom both of her parents had wanted. But if we knew all that the future was to hold, the world would be too much. Cara's mother would one day leave her at a time most vulnerable for a young girl. The day her mother died she was an afraid and inconsolable eleven-year-old, who cried herself to sleep. Life was made too fragile for Cara, and her confidence never returned. When her father remarried, there was no love for her and no room for her in her stepmother's world, and her father sent her to live with her grandparents. Though a grandmother's love waited for her and enveloped her, and took her as her own, the security she had known in her parental home before her mother died never returned. Now she was twice abandoned.

In the foreign service expatriates club, there were few secrets. It was a fishbowl world of direct contact, still without the internet, cell phones, and texting. There was a NATO vs non-NATO camaraderie in the early days of political change. Cara's marriage was not the only marriage put to the test; it was just one of the first to be put to the test. It would be played out for all to see in the Club where she and her husband were never quite accepted as equals by the state department folks, or the commercial expats who worked at higher levels. It was a bitter and separating event for Cara, from both her husband and from the community. For her husband, it was a choice to stay with his wife, or go to the young woman pregnant with his child. Cara had a more bitter choice. She was humiliated to try to cling to her marriage if it were possible to be saved, or to be both humiliated and alone, and unloved for the third time.

The M7 highway west of the capital city runs northeast to southwest, to the great inland freshwater lake. Along this corridor, traffic crosses the countryside each day and fills the highway. The fields extend on either side of the highway to the horizon – great fields with crops grown on huge state-owned cooperative farms. When we first arrived to live here, men still cut part of the fields with scythes. Beyond the lake where the road narrows to two lanes, there are kilometers and kilometers of fields along both sides of the road. Between the villages and petrol stations, there are rest stops for coffee and palinka brandy which dot the countryside. In the east of the country on the other side of the capital, the great plains of the puszta run all the way to the distant border of the birch-forested Ukraine.

A lone church steeple rises to the north of the highway as you approach the city from the west. Finally, the heroic Soviet statue of Kapitány Osztapenko appears between the east and west lanes of the highway. He was killed in December 1944 by the Nazis, while attempting to negotiate the surrender of the city, after Hitler ordered a defense to the last man. Cara's husband came to this city forty-five years later, to capture and defend his own minor career struggle. Gazing at the lone church in the distance, and then the charging bronze figure with raised sword, he wondered if this city would be the place of his own defeat.

His daily commute gave him much time to reflect. At the end of each day, he entered the city, crossing Törökbálint west of the city centrum, through Budakeszi and the forested parks of Hüvösvölgy, to his home in the Második Kerület, the 2nd District. This was the area of embassy housing and expatriate homes, while the young woman filling his thoughts lived in a modest village where hundreds of years earlier lay claimed a palace throne. Now hers was a city crowned only with the commerce of a joint-venture company after the expiration of socialism.

"What are we going to do?" Cara cried to her husband each evening when he arrived home.

"This young girl you have been with is only a child herself, yet we have no children of our own. You would not give me a child, and now she has your child as well as your reputation! What will you do, what must we do to make this right? What will happen to us, what will the company do, what will your colleagues think of you, what will they think of me? How could you betray me like this, and humiliate me so far from home?"

"I feel abandoned all over again," she said finally, exhausted, to no one but herself.

We no longer saw Cara and her husband at the expatriate club, as rumors of their difficulty spread throughout the community. There would be no abortion, the girl would keep the baby. Though barely a woman, still a child, she knew what this chance meant, and though she was only a village girl, her parents, her friends, and even her priest recognized what this could mean to her and to the child. Distant relatives lived in the States. A hard life of limited education and job opportunities suddenly changed to a hopeful future as her life was lifted up.

Cara began her descent. She felt herself sink beneath the surface. She thought of her dead mother whom she had loved, and the father, step-mother, and husband whom she had tried to love in turn. She felt herself slip beneath waves of grief that began to overtake her with despair and the loss of hope.

The Vadaskert Hospital for Psychiatric Therapy and Suicide Prevention sits on a leafy hill in District II. Anyone passing through the District is able to see the imposing structure on the hill which centuries ago was a deer park for royalty called Leopold Meadow. It lays at the boundary of the city proper as the road turns to the northwest. We did not know until later that Cara was hospitalized in the Vadaskert. To us it was a leafy expanse in the city along the busy route north around the hills of the three borders mountain, the Hármashatár-hegy. From the mountain was a vista of the bridges with the beauty and bounty of the city, a vista from far enough away not to see the bullet riddled and shell pockmarked buildings still extant from the war in certain districts. Within the walls of the Vadaskert, Cara saw nothing but the emptiness of her own third abandonment, complete with the excrement of her grief with which she stained her hands, and painted the walls of her cell.

All of the expatriate lives went on as before. The men worked and played golf on weekend excursions, and the wives entertained themselves with the difficulty of shopping, and the time-consuming complexities of frequent vacation planning amidst a confusing mix of languages and currency. There was always someone coming into or going out of our expatriate community, and Cara's absence was hardly felt. Her rehabilitation in the Vadaskert was complete, and the divorce proceeded after the repatriation home. There would be a new wedding and a birth. Life goes on without any particular one of us. This was not the only marriage or life that had been damaged during our years abroad, not the only tragedy of sickness or death, not the only affair of the heart by the married or unmarried, by the foreigner or by the national.

It is the painted box that haunts me, and Cara's two-word handwritten note inside. It was Cara's parting gift to me that I think of now, always, whenever I open a wooden desk box, a side table decoration, or something to put on a bookcase shelf. I wonder if she thought of it, too, that evening when she drove to the fields and parked. Always polite and fastidious so as not to disturb or to be a bother to anyone else – not to be the inconvenient eleven-year-old child after her mother died, the unwanted child that she was to the step-mother when her father re-married, nor to be the vengeful wife betrayed by her husband for a younger woman. She walked away from her immaculate car, into the field. Now only her shoes were a bit dirty, and in a few moments, would also be her knees.

I will always wonder, if her last thought in this world, was the same as the one she wrote to me, on the note she left in that little wooden box; when she knelt into the earth, cried a last time for her long dead mother, and put the barrel of the gun into her mouth, before she closed her eyes and pulled the trigger.

"remember me"

17.
The King of Cseresznyés Palacsinta

Water leaking in all the WCs, I swear. You need to step carefully. If it is bad enough there might be a wooden pallet across the floor to stand upon, at least something to keep your feet dry and out of the water.

I step out onto the balcony and it is pleasant enough here. On this late spring evening the weather is temperate and mild, and here in the countryside, the humidity has not yet descended upon the village in the way it has already begun to in the densely populated capital. At least the air is clean here, except for the coal smell that hangs in the air in winter time, and in late spring now there is no coal burning.

I am in a socialist party hotel, like all the other hotels in the countryside. It is too far from Balaton to house the vacationing workers who are on holiday there, but the provincial city is close enough, and there are many government-run businesses in the vicinity, industrial and agricultural, many serving the food and beverage industry.

I will be in the factory tomorrow, the largest employer in this part of the country, multiple buildings in a single site, some crumbling and needing major repairs, and others being newly built beside them, as the former state-owned venture tries to pull itself together into the post-modern world. The nearby blue lagoon of a certain chemical hue, will have to be cleaned and decontaminated from the decades of wastes placed into it, which were stored there in the open air. The Comicon economy still holds sway, the Soviet Council for Mutual Economic Assistance, but it is rapidly diminishing, or at least being displaced by market driven forces as walls and curtains fall everywhere.

Tonight, on this balcony, I want to let all of that go. I hear the clip-clop of horse's hooves on the path across the ravine onto which I overlook, from my balcony at the back of my hotel.

Suddenly, to my astonishment, the sound of a Russian MIG fighter jet screams in the sky above the hotel and across the ravine, heading west to the Croatian border, to threaten the hot war there before it turns back east, erasing the sound of the horse's hooves and bringing me back to where I am, and why I am here. The Búcsú Nap, Farewell Day, will not yet occur for another year, and then the Russian soldiers will be gone.

I have not heard roosters crowing in the morning since I was a small boy on my grandfather's farm. But here I awaken to their call, and dress and go down to the breakfast room where bread and hard rolls, and butter and jam, sliced meats, cheese, an assortment of fruit juices, and soft-boiled eggs if you want them wait for me. And urns of delicious, thick, black coffee.

In this country you will work with people who graduated from this country's own universities, many of whom have never been out of the country, or further than the next bordering country within the former curtained wall. Later, you will see some of them progress to levels above your own as they grow older with new experience, and you will feel the pride of having been there when the sound of the horse's hooves was still accompanied by the Russian MIGs.

This will come later. This night, after work, when you are at the weekend house of your colleague from the factory, you cannot imagine that far ahead. Now it is simply a blind fear of failure and of the unknown, in a place you do not recognize, but somehow you do recognize the people. It is like a strange dream where you cannot understand what is being said in the language around you, though you know who the people are, and what they should be saying.

The grape roots behind the tiny house are planted on a hillside so steep it is hard to keep your balance when you try to stand still. The vines hold grapes which have already begun to ripen in the warming sun captured on this hillside of late spring. We go into the cellar, and round glass vials with long tubes are dipped into wooden barrels and white wine is drawn out and taken upstairs, but not before some of it is streamed into our open mouths, drawn from the barrels into the glass vials, with the long tubes then held high above our heads and released.

It is the cherries for which we have come into the house on this warm June evening, and at first, I do not know it, because we have been looking at the grapes and visited the barrels in the cellar. There will be singing with János, István, Imre, and Tamás, while Ján's wife, wrapped in a white apron, makes the cherry pastries, the cseresznyés palacsinta, on the cooktop in the corner of the room, with her back turned to us.

The men sing and mourn the Battle of Mohács, where King Lajos II drowned trying to cross Csele Creek to the north and escape, defeated by the Ottoman Empire's Suleiman the Magnificent in 1526. Faces red with wine, backs held straight away from the chairs, chests thrust high above the table, heads held proud and erect, arms are pushed forward holding glasses filled with wine, as the verses of an ancient song proceed to tell the story of a nation defeated but proud, of history alive almost five hundred years hence, but never forgotten.

We stagger out of the small Wochenendhaus to the waiting driver and car. All the weekend houses look the same to me in the darkening twilight, and I cannot tell where I have been or where I am going. The branches of the shrubs lining the dirt path with grass growing in the center, scrape the sides of the car as we pass by the gardens that grow in front of every small structure. Taken back to my room at the hotel, I am dizzy with the wine and the singing, and the richness of the pastries, and the homesick feeling I have at night when I open the balcony door and look out upon this strange, ancient land.

I fall asleep and imagine the clip-clop of horse's hooves, the screaming of a fighter plane, the clamor of battle, the raising of a glass, a woman's white apron, fires and songs, the sweet taste of cherries, and exhausted, the bitter failure, of a long-ago king.

18.

Beneath the Balboa Tree of Guescheme

"The baby, where is the baby? Do you have the baby? They go down to the babies. I want the baby. Because of the babies. What do you want the baby for? Do you have the baby?"

"Where is the baby?"

Now she quieted herself, and rubbed her hands together. The scar on her left hand, on the fleshy part between her thumb and forefinger was rubbed almost raw.

"Mary Ellen," said the nurse's aide, "don't hurt yourself, let me put some cream on your hands."

"What do you see? Do you see her? What did you do?" Mary Ellen continued, looking up as if trying to find something, and then for a moment she was silent.

"Where are you? Who are you? I like you. I don't know you. One, two, three, four, five, six, seven, eight. One, two, three, four, five, six, seven, where is the baby? Is that the baby? Where is the baby? I don't know. I don't know why I don't know. I don't know why it is so hard. What is it? I don't remember. I don't know. She is just a baby. I have never. It's on the nose. What nose? It's on the baby. I'm not going to go, because I don't want to go. I don't know if I can do it."

"Oh, Mary Ellen, you can do it. Let's go back to your room. Dinner is over, let's move away from the table."

"Where is the baby? Do you have the baby? One, two, three, four, five, six, seven, eight. One, two, three, four, five, six, seven. Where are the babies? I lost the baby. I don't know where the baby is."

Down the hall an old man cried as the nurse turned on the water.

"I'll make it warm for you, Charlie, don't worry, it won't be cold. You'll like it"

"No, no, no, no," he cried. "Oh no, no, no, no, no, no, no-ooo."

His cries intensified as she began to splash the water on his feet and legs.

"Oh no," he cried and waved his arms about him.

I had to hold his arms so that he could not move away.

"Oh no, no, no-ooo."

The nurse took his hands and ran water over his fingers and his palms, but his head remained bowed. He sat on the shower seat with his back bent over and he did not look at the hand that held his, nor up to meet the nurse's kind face.

"I have to wash you, Charlie, you'll feel better. Here, see? Stand up and let me wash you. The water feels good, it's warm, it's not too cold, and it's not too hot."

"And then we will put your pajamas on, and you will feel clean, and you can relax and go to bed and sleep."

His cries stopped, and she washed the aged body of a ninety-six-year-old man. This was the only thing he ever complained about, and it took two of them to get him into the bathroom for a sit-down shower. The only other words he ever said to anyone was, "Thank you." There was no fat on his body and though the muscles were shrunken, his skin did not hang loose on his frame. He had the look of someone who had known physical labor, the lack of body fat of a boxer, now a spirit descending but he was still fighting, and he had a fear of water, but we did not know why.

"Do you know what happened to Mary Ellen," I asked. "Something must have happened to her that makes her talk the way she does."

"I don't know. They say her husband was a sweetheart, was always so kind to her when he visited, but he died last year.

Someone said he was a missionary before they met and were married, and they had no children of their own. Now there is no one to visit her. It's sad."

She dried off the old man, gently rubbed his body with the towel, and I helped him sit down. I dressed him while she cleaned up the shower area and put the towels and his dirty clothes into a pile in the corner of the bathroom. We both left the room and went down the hall to tend to the next resident.

"Each night the Bori worshipers appeal to the in-dwelt demons of the Balboa tree outside our missionary huts. None of the people that come to our clinic will stay in the in-patient hut that is closest to the tree. They believe that the spirits are in the branches and the roots," the missionary wrote to the Women's Church Circle back home.

"It distresses us so to see the women of the village take part in these un-Christian rituals. They are not as strong Muslims as the people of other villages. The women, especially, take part in this demon worship. We hope that we might reach them for the sake of their souls, and turn them away from the pagan Bori rituals. At times they seem so bound to Satan – how distressing it is for us to see! In a continent where the sun has such strength, we hope that we might turn them from darkness into the light of Christ, like the night which turns to the brilliant days of African sunshine, which washes over everything with the power to heal or harm."

"My journey this time, dear friends, began so precipitously with the confusion first of my flight from New York, then the problem in Paris where I had no companion with which to share my two-day delay. I finally arrived on the African continent and could share in the good cheer of my Baptist hosts, before I trans-shipped on the mission plane from Niamey to Dosso. It was my great luck, and it was indeed a blessing to find the other nurse from our mission there waiting, as she had brought out one of the girls on furlough. I was able to travel with her in the midwife's Land Rover on the final leg of my journey, through the deep sand which fills the road from Dosso to Guescheme. I had now traveled nearly six thousand miles from where you sit reading this letter, dear friends, and with this news I hope to keep you close to me in spirit that you might help me with your prayers and thoughts. I must try to complete the work at hand over which we have prayed, for which we have collected alms, and for that which we have made out the greater purpose of our lives, so that we undertake to accomplish our Savior's work each day in our own way and in our own place."

"I was blessed to have Dije and Yohan with me for a month after my return here. When Dije had to go back to Galmi, Yohanna wanted to stay with me here, although he is still only five years old. I pray that he will one day become a true servant of the Lord."

"Blessings continue to follow us here. On the day before Dije left a group of women came to the dispensary, one with a tiny newborn child on her back. It was only ten days old and weighed only three pounds. The mother died on the way to the dispensary while traveling with the other women. I gave a bottle of milk to Dije and told her to teach them how to feed the baby. But later that day the men came, and they told us that we needed to keep the baby. We have named her Rahila, a Muslim name meaning, "one who travels," and she has done well. Soon our little Rahila will double her weight. Pray for this child, too, that she may grow up to one day also serve the Lord. Praise be to God."

"A ritual is being prepared for eight young girls who are maidens in this village, between the ages of nine and ten who live here within this clearing in the bush. These dear little ones, my babies, are in their preparation to become one with the women of their tribe. We must give them patience, and we will strive to instill in them Christian virtues amidst the demons that dwell among and in the hearts of the Muslim elders. We have been unable to reach these women so that they may let go of the

Bori worship for the sake of their children, even with the example of our Lord's pain and suffering, and his sacrifice given up to save them."

"I have not yet witnessed this ritual, a cleansing it has been described to us, and a cultural rite of passage, the details of which we have been told we might not understand. But the elders have shown Christian-like solicitude for their children, in that they have asked us to bring new medicines so that they rely not only on traditional healing. It pleases us that they have asked for balms. Where we have not reached the soul, perhaps through our concern for their bodily health, we may yet reach them through healing. We have come here as you know, dear friends, to save souls with your blessed help and support. Perhaps we may reach the souls of these outstretched hands, after our medicines have helped to heal their children. But the task is difficult, pray for me to have the strength to complete my duties and witness this rite of passage in which we have been invited to participate for the first time. We feel that this witness is a symbol of the trust which we are working to forge between our missionaries and the villagers, through Christ our Lord, amen."

"Kwaha and Halilu will visit us from the Bible school at Aguia during Christmas, then Hodi and Gwanna will enter it in the New Year. Pray that these may all be completely dedicated to the Lord, though Gwanna is only a Christian for one year, and does not yet read well."

"Finally, Sahiro and his wife Abshe continue to do well at our little Church in Guescheme. Remember that these were saved at our Leprosarium, and attended the Aguia school."

"Dear friends, I must post this letter today as the commencement of this ritual will take place tomorrow, and since as you know the post is collected only one day per week. I will complete the description of this ritual in my next letter to you, with God's grace and joy, and the knowledge that our Christian beliefs and missionary efforts are making a difference on this beautiful continent, for these people who live simple lives of a great and ancient culture so unlike our own."

"I will write again, soon, my dear community of believers, to relate my witness of the experiences in which I am blessed to be able to take part."

The next day one of the women elders took the girls from the quarantine or isolation hut, and sat them down under the Balboa tree. Its branches spread over the dusty earth packed from the feet of all the tribesmen and women who had gathered under its canopy over the generations it had lived among them. The time of their learning would soon be over, these young girls were to soon become women of this village, which was surrounded by the bush and the culture of a thousand years. Colorful fabrics were spread on the ground beneath the girls as they sat obediently in front of the elder, on the other side of the tree away from the eyes of the men and boys, and the other women of the village. The missionary women would be permitted to witness this sacrament as it had been explained to them, an African sacrament as necessary to their culture, as the Christian sacraments were for the morality and personal cleanliness which came from their Lord, beginning with the ten commandments.

It would be a baptism of sorts, the purpose or practice of which was yet unknown. Still, the missionaries were asked to bring the medicines seen in the missionary clinic. There were decorative scars visible on many of the villagers as part of other rituals, and now the drugs were brought to the elder woman who stood before the girls.

Then a most strange thing happened, and disturbing to witness by standards of Christian chastity and modesty. The girls were undressed, removing their skirts and underclothes and they lay down on their backs on the fabrics beneath them, spreading out their legs, bent at the knees like frogs, a row of innocent children lying in the shade beneath the tree. The elder inspected each of them in turn, noting the size or shape of each girl, and whether the "nose" was long or short, fleshy or rounded. Later, the woman elder would consult with the parents of each girl, and together they would decide what was best, and what was to be done, and she in turn received her fee based on what was agreed upon. The girls sat up, giggling to each other, and teasing one another as they dressed, and ran back to their parents, to play, to their chores, to their schoolwork.

"Dear Diary, would that I could have written this to my friends in the letter just posted two days ago, but you must suffice for me this night as I am beyond myself with puzzlement and fear and embarrassment of the intimacy which I have just witnessed. I know of the Jewish practice for boys, and the following of many Gentiles as well. I had thought, were these girls to be marked somehow with a ritual scar? Was this to be a cleansing ritual for girls who had not yet entered womanhood?"

The ceremony would take place on the second day, after all of the men and boys left the village for their own day of masculine rituals, of hunting and tracking, and crossing the river.

"In the morning I awoke to the sound of blades being sharpened, straight ones, and scissors, and strangely shaped ones, almost like scoops. One by one, the girls were undressed and bathed. They began to tremble, and I began to pray for strength to participate in this native religious ceremony which I was about to witness for the first time, charged as I am myself to witness and to bring the light of Christ to this African village."

The missionary remembered the muted cries and moans of the young girls, one by one, and then nothing more. She was barely able to endure the sight of the first cutting that she witnessed. The "nose" of the first girl was small, and there was little flesh on her intimate parts. The knife flashed quickly on top of her, as the same elder woman who had examined her the day before completed her excision without anesthetic, and then applied the clinic's antiseptic with which she had been provided. The second girl was more fully developed, and her parents had decided that more help was required. The elder cut quickly at first, then with writhing cries the girl suffered excision of all of her fleshy parts, and the stitching together as well, so that for her future wedding night she would have to be cut open again. The missionary was unable to bear witness to this additional procedure, and shaken, left the side of the woman elder and the children, and retired to her hut, horrified at what she had seen. In her mind she mixed the bleeding images of the girls with the bloody images of her Lord's suffering and crucifixion, and this did not console her. She fell into a deeply disturbed, unconscious sleep, which did not assuage her weariness nor restore her strength.

Later, the next day, the missionary emerged from her hut having gathered anything she could of her small possessions, to make gifts for each of the eight girls, except one. There were now only seven healing girls, who passed that day to an African womanhood.

She visited the woman elder, who had performed this annual ritual once again, one of many times in this village, careworn after a difficult day of solemn responsibility. Still cleaning her instruments, the elder thanked the missionary for the medicines she had provided. Fewer girls would die, with the use of the antiseptics which the missionaries brought with them from America.

"Dear Diary, one last cut was made today. I took one of the knives from the woman elder, and cut myself in the fleshy part between the thumb and forefinger of my left hand."

Only one girl would die that day from the complication of septic shock and hepatitis.

"Today I helped to bury Ntsoaki Ntŝeno, whose name means, "a girl between two boys." She was buried with both Christian and African rituals. Her older brother had been the first in her family to go to 2nd school."

"As we cut her, I now cut myself, to make an African scar that I will take to my own grave, and with which I will remember "the girl between two boys" the rest of my days. In the name of the Lord, our Savior, forever and ever in His service. Amen."

19.
The Orchard

The brothers sat under the shade of the poplar trees surrounding the old orchard. The trees reached above them into the sky, a blue shimmering cerulean in the summer heat of July. They dragged two chairs from the porch of the old farmhouse across the meadow to sit in the summer shade and talk. The burying was done, a long history concluded, and now was their time to quietly reminisce about the past, to sit quietly in the midst of the old unpruned trees and think about what was so long ago, and what might still be in their different lives. One had left the farm and the history of that part of Germany long ago, the other yet behind, still cleaving to the past, a tangled ball of thread with the elders of the family. Now the old farmhouse was quiet with the loss which magnified his own.

"Yes, but you see," said the elder, who had returned to complete the circle, "there were many things different then, and I knew that I must leave and suffer both the leaving and the coming into the new world which did not welcome me."

"It's not the same, you see, when you remember the farm as a child. When morning and evening the animals need tending, the rain turns the fields to mud which reaches your ankles, and the stalls need to be cleaned. In the summer the flies bite your face and neck and arms, the sun burns your face, and in the wintertime the cold seeps into your boots until your feet are numb. It is one discomfort or another depending on the season."

The schoolmates knew which of those who came from the farms, by the clothes, or by the white that started where the skin had been covered from the sun.

"And here you are still, twenty-five years after."

U.S. Major General Emil Reinhardt's 69th Infantry Division of the 1st Army V Corps rolled through this region in April 1945 where they met Major General Vladimir Rusakov of the Russian 58th Guards Infantry Division. Soon after, the entire region was turned over to the Red Army to become East Germany at the end of the war.

Their mother had lived through Weimar, the Nazis, the Americans, and the Russians, and finally after unification, the truly German. Her life was a succession as much as were the neighbors who changed in the lands surrounding the farmhouse. The politics had repeatedly changed over the years, but the fields of the farm did not. The truth of that remained the same. Now all of that which had happened was done, and the burying, too, was past.

The elder brother continued.

"It was not easy to leave and go to the west, though in fact Bavaria is in the south. It is one of the peculiarities you see, that the direction was one thing and the meaning another, but I knew, correctly, where I needed to be. I had had enough. I would exceed the provincialism of the farm, the town, and the abuse of my schoolmates by going to places they would not see, and to speak languages they could not understand. I needed to expand and would not be held back by the contraction of their taunts and ridicule. And yet I have never been able to hide the size and strength of my hands, and feet sturdy enough to work the farm. My back was too strong for the library but that is where I found myself. I excelled against those who disbelieved, and many for a long time thought it was not where I belonged."

The younger brother sat silently beside the older one. He knew this was not a reproach on his life, but a censure which the older had not allowed to remain on his own. The younger had never felt thus, and perhaps was sheltered from a sensitivity which the older brother felt, that he did not possess. It would not be perceived by him. After all, he was still here, and the meadow which they had crossed, and the orchard in which they now sat were as much a part of him as his own hands, which into each other they now were cupped. He did not regret the staying, and would never feel the confusion, nor the sorrowful knowledge of a seeker.

"Well now you see," continued the elder, "what has become of me. Sitting here it is a puzzle as to who was left behind, and who did not remain."

The land changes gradually where the trains roll north and to the east from the foothills of the Alps. Vineyards lay on hills of groomed fields, which lie all the way to the city streets of the industrialized towns. Onward lie fertile fields flat and groomed, where every part of the land surrounding cities and villages is organized for use. As you travel north through Nuremberg and Bamberg, and east through Leipzig and beyond, you follow the tracks away from the south and head into the hills and valleys of the north. Now the further you travel, the less well-groomed the areas surrounding the fields and the lakes and the copses that embrace a farmhouse in the countryside, and the less well-groomed are the gardens of the weekend houses, gathered here and there. Perhaps this difference remained in the brothers, one more groomed and one less so, but how would you tell who was the one most exploited, and the one less so?

A bottle was opened, and the device passed to the other. The hiss of gas also escaped the second Radeberger. Nothing would change now; the brothers would go on as before. Perhaps the passing of a generation would settle long ago questions. The land would remain, one life tethered and one life free. The important thing was so simple, like the sitting in an orchard, and the taste of a pilsner. Perhaps there was no freedom and there was no tether. Perhaps the one who is tied is free, and the one who is free is tethered.

"Yes, but you see." the elder said.

And, "It is not the same." he paused.

"And here you are still."

20.
Rabbit Hunting

The road out of town went past the city park. The countryside lay beyond, and the hill that marked the top of the park lay above the town like a sentinel. Green spaces of the town itself bordered the park for acres on the side of the park that faced the town, so that it was separated itself, though still part, of the town. On the other side of the park lay the farm fields. You could still see over the tops of the evergreen trees then, for they had not yet overgrown and taken the view away, the trees that ringed the top of the park just below the crest of the hill, like the tonsure of a monk's haircut. On the side of the park facing the city you could see west, south, and east over the rooftops and trees of the former canal town. The spires of its churches pierced the canopy of the trees, letting you know which streets you were looking at, and at what intersection of the town, like a surveyor calling out the distances and directions of a plot being measured.

He lived just outside the green space bordering the park. He put the shell into the inside pocket of his hunting vest, and lifted the shotgun from its case. His father was born on a farm, and when he or his grandfather went to hunt it was only off the front porch of their farmhouse and into the fields or into the woods. There was no longer a farm house in the family but it pleased him to know that from his home he could still walk to the fields and woods outside of the town during hunting season. It was pleasant to leave the house and cross the green space and walk to the top of the park, and on out into the countryside to hunt with the permission of the farmers he knew. It was pleasant to drink his coffee at the bare wooden kitchen table, and only hear the clink of the shells where they rattled in his pocket, or the sound of the breech of the gun when he picked it up and checked to see that it was not loaded, and not to hear the sound of an engine starting. He could walk and did not need the extra burden of a car.

It was not unusual in that time to see men carrying rifles or shotguns in hunting season at the edge of the town that bordered the countryside. Or from the cars or pick-up trucks that were parked on roadsides near the fields and woods where hunting was permitted. It had been that way all his life, like the men you could see walking the mile or two from their homes to the mills where they worked, their lunch pails swinging by their sides. People still walked then. Every small town had a bus or streetcar line, and it was not unusual to see people on the street. Even with their hunting guns in 1961.

It was just before sunrise, on a cool November morning, a light rain precipitated overnight, enough to dampen everything, and the rabbits would be moving at sunrise to dry themselves in the sun. He knew this, and though it was a work day, he knew his wife would understand why he would leave so early, and that he would also return to change clothes and to go to work later in the morning. His father and grandfather had hunted all their lives, though he had been able to hunt much less so. After an early coffee he left the house. It pained him not to say goodbye to his children, but it was better this way. They needed their sleep and would leave for school after he was gone and in the field. He knew he needed to be there, in the field this morning.

He left the house and walked beyond the last street of the neighborhood, and was at the edge of the green space that lay before the park. He could walk by the side of the road, or cut across the field. Already he could feel the pull away from the town and the paved places and the people that he knew, and he crossed the ditch and entered the parkland border below the hill. Here the grass had been cut, and though it was wet it was not long, and it did not reach beyond the tops of his boots. A few cars were coming to town from the road on the other side of the park, none yet going back out into the countryside.

The last time he had hunted with his father they kicked out only one rabbit, and it was his father who saw it first, raised the gun to his shoulder, and fired, with the smoothness of motion of one who had hunted all his life. Either startled or hit, the rabbit tumbled in front of itself, but it had not been hit, and it somersaulted back onto its feet, disappeared into the long grass, and was gone. Today he told himself over and over, he would not miss, so that he needn't think about it anymore, and he walked up to the crest of the park's hill and over to the other side. At the bottom of the hill on the other side of the park, he crossed a fence and entered the hunting field.

Almost everyone in a town like that knew the man who had the kind of job he had. It is a small-town blessing or curse. It is not so for the working men who carried their lunch pails on the sidewalks for their walk to and from the mills. Their lives are known only on the shop floors. But Henry worked in a professional capacity in a business that served the public. All would know he had been rabbit hunting. All would know what happened that morning.

A shot from the field was heard in the farm house that lay next to the road.

"Someone is out early this morning," said his wife, as she spooned the boiling lard over his eggs, the edges turning brown and the yolks skimming over.

"It might be Henry," said her husband, a mug of coffee in his hand.

"He told me if the weather cleared, he'd be out this week while it's early in the season. Fine, I told him, maybe he'll bring us something for a stew."

There was only one shot, then silence from the field. It was six-thirty, a few minutes after dawn, and a half hour before the sunrise.

"I reckon he got it," said the wife, taking the eggs out of the pan for her husband, and not hearing a second shot in quick succession.

"How many strips of this bacon do you want?"

And glancing out the window, saw nothing in the distance but the clearing mistiness of a sunrise already beginning to brighten the southeastern sky.

Miss Stiles' third grade class at Main Street Elementary School came to order at eight-thirty in the morning. The boys tried to settle down, and the girls tried to shush them. The boys still thought of summer vacation, which had ended less than two months before, the girls thought about the boys, and the Thanksgiving and Christmas holidays which would soon arrive, and the preparations they were already anticipating. The teacher called the class to order, made a note of attendance, and began the pledge of allegiance to the flag, as the children stood and put their right hands over their hearts.

She loved the beginnings of the mornings, when the boys were still quiet and not yet fully awake, and the girls fussed with their clothes and the young voices repeated the words with only the innocence that children can evoke. It was a beautiful autumn morning, and her classroom faced south, with the bank of windows catching the early morning light which seemed to help awaken the faces of the children. Directly outside her window, the American flag waved in the breeze, because the sixth-grade flag boys raised it on the pole before class began each day. All the boys in each class hoped to have this honor when they were older, and to be able to unfold, raise, bring down, and fold the flag again at the end of the day, with the thrill of its going up each morning, and seeing the glances of the girls watching them, and the responsibility of taking it down each day, and folding it as properly as a soldier. The teacher, Miss Stiles, looked out over her children as they finished the pledge within site of the flag outside, and the morning sun began to brighten the classroom.

The father never returned from the field that morning, and there would be no rabbit left at the back door for the farmer's wife to make into stew.

I still remember the quiver in Miss Stiles' voice after she had gone to the office to see the principal, and returned to take Henry's son from the room. I sat in a row farther back from him, he was closer to the window, and I still remember his silhouette against the light from the windows of our room, and how quiet it had become when Miss Stiles put her arms around his shoulders and told him that he needed to go home. I still remember her gentleness, more like a mother than the unmarried teacher that she was. We had been in the middle of our arithmetic lesson, and I was already thinking about the walk home for lunch, and the hot potato soup that my mother would make from scratch and have waiting for me. It was flash card arithmetic time, and Bert Ruttlier had correctly answered eight cards in a row before he stumbled on the ninth and sat down. I would only learn later that the world did not always add up.

No one ever talked about what happened that morning in the rabbit field beyond the park. We did not understand, and did not know how to ask questions about what had taken place, when the father knelt down against the muzzle of the gun, and left the world, and his family, and my third-grade class.

21.
The French Professor

A tennis court is seventy-eight feet long, and twenty-seven feet wide for singles play. You must put the ball into play on or within the service line which is twenty-one feet from the net. It is not an easy game to play within the lines. Perhaps it is like life – if you hit the ball hard, you must know how to play a spin on it to keep it within the lines. You cannot take your eye off the ball, and you must follow it all the way into the racket, at the same time knowing where you want to hit it, and directing it with the kinesthetic knowledge in your muscles, a knowledge achieved with repetitive practice and experience. If you hit the ball too hard, and do not apply enough spin to make the ball dive back down within the lines, it will go out and your opponent will win the point.

Tennis used to be a gentleman's game. During play, if you saw that your own ball touched outside of any part of the two-inch wide white line, but your opponent did not, you were obliged to call it out, even in a match ruled by a referee if he did not see it go out. It was expected that your opponent would do the same. This was before the modern era of the US Open after the players began to use racquets not made out of wood. The men began to argue calls to the point of forfeiting a match, with the introduction of rough language and discourteous behavior. The white clothes of Wimbledon remained, but the culture and observation of the honor code did not.

I had never before played tennis with Frances. We had never participated together in any physical activity, and it was a warm late spring day at the university. In fact, I had never before seen her outside of class, though from the first time I heard her speak the French language she interested me. I would see her three times a week for the better part of a year, and sometimes we talked together after class if we had time, but it was always about the class and the learning, and the love of the sound and feel of the language. Actually, she more than interested me. But I could never imagine that things could go beyond a class discussion. I could not believe it would have been possible for her to become my girlfriend. She was my French professor.

I was still a strong player, now a college graduate living on the east coast, and I played with friends who had been college tennis and lacrosse players, very good college athletes. I was a natural at tennis, and though I never played a team match again after I graduated from high school, I was competitive with these friends who had played in college. I had declined an invitation to join the formal sport in order to concentrate on my university studies and my girlfriends, among them both were French for a time, and which would eventually bring me to this day on the court.

In fact, I was with a tennis player friend and sometimes companion, who was with me the morning I received the letter inviting me to join an honorary society in a ceremony to be held at my former university. I did not understand what the invitation was for, nor what the organization represented, and I threw it away. It was she who retrieved it from the waste basket, having emerged from the bedroom as I went through the mail. I laughed at the university correspondence, the importance of which I did not understand. And though it is true I did not understand what it was that my friend retrieved from the waste basket, I had learned to pay attention to whatever it was she had to say, when this smart and beautiful woman walked across the floor of my apartment wearing nothing but a satisfied morning smile.

She pushed me down onto the sofa, straddled me, pulled my face between her breasts and explained that I could not turn down this offer, or she would smother me against her body. Of course, I acquiesced only after she pressed my face against her and I needed to breathe. So that was how it all began. A beautiful player tossed the ball in my direction, and I hit it over the net and tried to keep the ball in play within the lines.

I sent in my acceptance and began to plan my trip back to the university. I decided to contact my French professor who still lived and taught there, and told her I would soon be visiting the grounds again. I thanked her for all the help she had given me in class, and how much I had enjoyed learning the language she taught. I knew that my success in her classes helped enable me to receive this honor. She was generous enough to agree to come to the auditorium and meet me there, and attend the ceremony with me. She suggested that if the weather was nice, and if we had time, we should do something fun to celebrate. She asked me if we could play a set or two of tennis, as she was learning the game and she somehow remembered that I also played. Perhaps we had discussed the language of the sport at one time in class, because the language building and classrooms were in sight of the university courts.

After the ceremony, I walked to my hotel on Main Street and dressed for tennis while she went to change clothes in her office at the foreign language building.

It is always a bit awkward when you play tennis with someone for the first time. It is a sport which requires a certain degree of skill to play well, and I do not like to play with someone if I do not know how well they play. With my friends it was easy, you just did not play together if you were not at the same skill level or at least close. It's not fun to chase balls hit over the fence that surrounds the court, or play a lopsided match if every well-hit ball becomes a sure winner. Very seldom did I play against a woman who was not a good player, it is just not a fun date game, if one plays well and the other does not.

We met at the courts on Main Street, and walked over to the bench which sat in the middle of the court beside the net.

"Tu dois être fiers de ton succès," she smiled, and she took my hand and kissed me first on the left, and then on the right cheek.

"You must be proud of your success, félicitations," she said and we sat down.

I felt so much older and more at ease than I ever did when I was a student in class in the language building nearby, or when I was hitting balls for exercise on the courts at which we now sat. No longer a student, now we were both adults, though I had only been away for one year.

"I brought two cans of balls," I said, "so we do not have to chase the ones that get away at every point."

A satisfying whoosh left the first can as I pulled the tab to open it.

"Does that mean you expect me to hit all of my shots out of the court?" she replied.

She looked at me with the same expression of laughter around her eyes that I remembered from class when I did not quite pronounce something correctly, or mixed up a sound which gave a completely different meaning, and she pursed her lips into a smile in the way that I also remembered.

I pulled the tab on the second can, and another "whoosh" escaped, as satisfying as the first.

"Well," I replied, "it's not that I don't trust you, maybe I don't trust myself!" I laughed.

It was fun now to be so close to her here on the court, so different from being in class, sitting here in the sun, wearing shorts and t-shirts, and ready to play a game where the object is to hit between the lines, knowing that it is almost impossible to do so, laughing out loud and seeing her smile outside of class and the language building for the first time. And for the first time she was not my professor, now she was my friend, and we would soon be doing an activity which would cause us, for the first time, to exert a physical effort together, not just an intellectual one.

She took a ball and dropped it on the ground, and then turning towards it, flicked her wrist with the racquet on the top of the ball and it bounced back into her hand. And then she did it with another one.

She looked at me and smiled at my surprise.

"Let's play," she said.

The lines around her eyes laughed at me with her smile.

"And maybe if we have time afterwards, and if you do not mind, we could go back to your hotel to get cleaned up and change, and have coffee somewhere before we both go home."

"Do you mind if I serve first?" she asked.

I was momentarily distracted by what she had said and the balls of the second can fell out as she said this, hit my shoes, and scattered over my side of the court. She laughed and walked across the court to stand on the right side of the center tape behind the service line, and I ran to pick up the balls and take my place on the other side of the court behind the back line to receive her serve.

A little more than a year had passed since my last language class with her, and now we were playing a game of tennis together at the university where I had studied, and at which she still taught. The language building was not far from view. It gave me a sense of accomplishment to have arrived here once again, not as a student but now as a graduated alumnus, fêted for an hour in the earlier afternoon, now standing on the court with the professor who was now my friend.

She played well, you could tell that she was taking lessons, as her movements were precise and still somewhat mechanical, not quite fluid yet, as there had not been enough time for her muscle memory to have settled into her movements, and make them more fluent. But she ran well and ably stopped and turned and moved against the balls, and her legs were well muscled, not too slender in her tennis shorts, which would have shown a lack of strength. It appeared that she must have played other sports when she was younger. Just a few years older than me, she had maintained that strength and conditioning well. She laughed aloud at each point won or lost, and she kept score precisely. She would not give up a point easily without a fight. She enjoyed the sport and the competition for sport's sake.

I had been playing the game since I was a boy, and I could be hard to beat in a match because although I knew it was only a game, I did not like to lose, and did not think twice about always trying to win. It was just a game, but it was most fun when your opponent tried as hard as they could to beat you. I did not think I would lose one game in the two sets we agreed to play. To my surprise, though I certainly would win each set, I did not win all of the games.

She was pleased with her performance and so was I, because we were able to rally together for points, and not just serve, hit, and win or lose a point when the ball moves just once or twice across the net. We were able to keep the ball in play more times than I had expected. It was obvious that she had taken lessons, and practiced hard to be able to play this game as well as she did, and I decided it should not have surprised me. She had gained a level of competence very efficiently because that is how she had always managed her life. It was why she was able to have the kind of life and career she now had. It was the first time I had known someone like her and was able to realize this truth. There are goals you can set for yourself throughout your life for things you want to achieve. Most people do not do this, for things both large and small. It is a paradox to some degree, because if you are single minded about goals, and inflexible to some degree in their pursuit, you may not notice or have time for things that come your way at random, sometimes wonderful things or people. And yet to achieve certain goals, some of these gifts along the way may have to be sacrificed in order to achieve and experience even greater gifts. Attainment and loss, and yet those who do not choose are left at the mercy of chance, and the occasional stranger.

We sat on the bench and toweled off, facing the sun for a few minutes with the warmth on our faces, feeling a satisfaction from the physical activity we had played together, quiet but not uncomfortable. We gathered up the balls, put them into the cans, and sat back down on the bench. There were a couple of players on the court on the other side of the fence from where we sat. The sound of a ball striking the strings of a tennis racquet is a very pleasant sound. The sounds came in quick succession from the two experienced players on the adjoining court.

"Our play did not sound like that," she said, "but we played well enough. I think we did very well together."

"Je ne suis pas fatigué, et toi? Let's sit here in the sun for a few minutes. I know you can't be tired, let's change and get a coffee. This was so much fun," she continued.

"It is so nice to see you again. I am so glad you are doing well. My god, I did not realize it was so hot and humid, I am soaked through!" she added.

"I'm glad I remembered to bring a couple of towels for us from my hotel. I never needed one in your class, although your tests did make my palms wet with stress!"

"I enjoyed this so much. Unless one of my students stays here for an advanced degree, I seldom keep in touch once they graduate. You always wonder how things work out for the students who make an impression on you. Is it the same for you with the training program you talked about at your company?"

"I haven't been there long enough to have experienced that yet, but you can tell who seems to be marked for success. Maybe it is like what you see in your classes. And it is not always the person with the highest grades in our training courses whom you think will be the most successful in the business, although it is always a factor for the people who stay in the company. Grades are a big part of the performance reviews you are given after each of your training classes and work assignments, and it does affect the subsequent jobs you are offered. And yet there are those you know who will be successful, but who do not fit in with the company's culture. Three of my favorite colleagues fit into that category. I know they will not stay with the company, but I also know they will all be successful. One will go to Wall Street, one to a small private foundation, and one will have a career in university sports management. I have only just begun to understand this.

They leaned back together to face the sun beneath a languid sky, and he drew the towel across his face one more time and put it down on top of his racquet. His left arm brushed against her right arm and she did not move nor open her eyes. Her lips did not move from the half smile she held on them.

They left the court and crossed the athletic fields where trees were planted in honor of the best athletes of years past, and crossed the pathways of the academical green. They walked past the library with the famous black and white optical illusion floor, with the not publicized but infamous brass railings on the open upper balconies, embedded with religious symbols to shock and to give notice in order to deter the inevitable, but thankfully rare jumper. It was pleasant walking through the grounds together, anticipating the comfortable atmosphere of the best coffee shop in the city, never visited by him with a professor, but always frequented by students and professors alike amidst the aroma of roasted coffee and pastries of the boulangerie café. It would be a short walk to the coffee shop from his hotel after they changed.

She went into the shower first and he tried to straighten up the room as best he could while he heard the water running. He had not expected her to be here. Her sports bag was dropped on the chair by the desk, casually unzipped and almost spilling its contents onto the carpet. She had not taken it into the bathroom.

Their tennis shoes were on the floor in front of the door, and her socks were on the floor in front of the chair. He put his towel on one of the chairs and sat down, removed his wrist band and socks, and threw them into his sports bag. Everything would be washed later.

He could hear the water running in the shower, and he got up and went to the refrigerator to get a bottle of water. He looked at the time, and sat down. The shower stopped and he heard the curtain open. He heard Frances' voice.

"Quelle merveilleux douche!" and she opened the bathroom door.

She came into the room wrapped in a white towel, her hair dripping wet, and she wrapped her hair up into another towel.

"Your turn," she said.

"I hope I did not use up all the hot water!" she teased.

Her eyes laughed and she pursed her lips. She took out clean clothes from her sports bag that she had left on the chair, put her tennis clothes into it, and dropped it onto the floor.

"I'm so thirsty," she said, "anything for me? I can't wait until we go for a coffee!"

For a moment as I went to the fridge to get another bottle of water, I did not know what to do. She walked over to me and her face was wet, and drops of water fell from her legs. The towel was wrapped loosely about her, and I could see the shape of her breasts partially covered with the top of the towel tucked into her side. She was beautiful, her face glowed from the exertion we had made in the sun, and the moistness of her skin. I was close enough to touch her when my hand and hers met on the bottle. I handed it to her, and she looked up into my eyes.

She laughed again, and with a gentle pull her towel dropped to the floor. She did not protest. She touched my face with her hand, and moved her right thumb across my lips.

"I'm so glad to see you again," and she reached up to kiss me, quickly.

"Don't take too long in the shower," she said, "but let's rest a bit before we go for a coffee."

I pulled off my shirt and removed my tennis shorts, and held her against me as I moved down then back up between her. I tried to push up against her and she did not resist, but she laughed again and turned to pick up her towel to dry off and shake out her hair. She went over and pulled the covers down off the bed.

I covered myself, not embarrassed, and went into the bathroom. Before I turned on the water, I could hear her voice in the room. She was singing something quietly to herself. I remembered that it was something from a recording she had played one day in class.

22.
The Hitchhiker

Dusk, late autumn, when the brilliant colors of the day gradually fade and turn to black and white, wrung out of the early evening like water before the laundry is hung out to dry. From the corner of my eye, I saw him by the side of the highway, where interstate hitchhiking is not allowed, down from the entrance ramp at the edge of the small, two stoplight town, walking down away from the entrance ramp onto the highway shoulder, not towards a broken-down car which I could not see. Dark pants, a dark hooded sweatshirt covering his head, walking easily, arms swinging loosely on the sides of his shoulders, away from the traffic, not even trying to get a ride. Fading sky and descending cold along the highway going north. Where was his car, where had he begun to walk? If he was walking up to one of the houses or cabins along the road, or to cross a field it made no sense. There was nothing nearby on the road ahead, the nearest gas station was a half mile behind him, nothing ahead of him for miles. The former camp was long gone, and paved over years ago.

In years past this was coal country, where strippers took the countryside and left it raw and un-reclaimed, with blue water pits where people came to dump their trash. You could go there with your high school friends to target shoot tin cans, and bottles, and rats if you saw them. No one minded the crack, crack, crack of the .22's, or if you carried one on the back seat of your car, or hung a rifle on the rack behind the bench seat of your pick-up truck. No one asked to see your ID if you bought a brick of five hundred rounds from the discount or hardware store, chances are they knew your father or mother anyway.

There were places where you could race your friends on the roads outside of small towns like this. This is the place where I first rode in a car going over a hundred miles an hour, holding onto the small back seat of a Fiat Sport Spider, trying to save my life from being flung out of that tiny convertible sports car with each bump in the road, and Timmy and Pete just laughing their heads off in front, the .22 in the trunk of the car on our way to the pits.

This was still a place then, where boys could hike into the fields with their friends and sleep under the stars looking for the Big Dipper and the North star, and drink pop and eat candy bars, and talk about girls all night while looking at your older brother's girlie magazines, and wake up in the morning with the cows grazing around you undisturbed by your presence in the pasture.

Soon it would be dark in-between the small towns of the on-and-off ramps of the highway along which the figure was now walking, where light would pierce the darkness only at the intersections of other highways. Years ago, I spent a night on a road like this, a cold embankment pressed against my back after the cop told me he'd arrest me if he found me back on the road again that night. And not enough money for both a hamburger and a coke, just water, in the joint across the road from the on-ramp where I had been stopped, searched, and left on the road. It was too late and too far to call for help at the pay phone. An unfriendly, unfortunate cop, probably unhappy at home who understood not his wife nor his children, nor my long hair and torn jeans which was all I had to wear, despite the academic graduation honors from the university I was traveling away from. It would be November of that year before I could afford to buy a warm winter coat to wear to the office of my first post-graduate job.

Something a little off in the way the figure walked, too easily, with arms swinging wide away from the body, as if the hands were rotated away with each forward motion and the forearms splayed outward, almost, but not quite feminine in shape and nature, and with a lightness in the motion, as if the walk was as easy and unconcerned as a casual walk in town. Dangerously, vulnerably alone, the sky fading to darkness to be illuminated only by the stars on the moonless night which was coming.

A moment's thought and I impulsively turned off the pavement, and pulled over to the side of the road onto the shoulder, and waited for the figure to overtake me. Like a time-machine and decades earlier, how I wished I had been helped on the road. I lowered the passenger window as the stranger approached. My girlfriend would not be happy if she knew I stopped to help a stranger this evening.

"Where are you headed, do you need a ride?" and almost to my surprise a woman's voice answered.

"Anywhere north, into the city near the lake there is a shelter there where I can stay for the night if I have to, or to any of the other main roads going east or west"

"Any weapons?"

"No."

I looked her over and could see by the cheap weight of her hooded sweatshirt that she had nothing on her person. She possessed nothing but a hollowness and fatigue. She gave the impression of a great undoing, a denouement of controlled fear and looked at me passively, as if resigned to accept whatever might be given or taken, now just a slight figure and there was no one else in sight. She was alone. How she ended up here, on the outskirts of this tired old town, I could not guess. I wondered what marks and bruises I could not see, physical or mental. But I asked her no more questions.

It used to be a vibrant place here, this country town surrounded by farms when it was an immigrant fueled backwater, where the brickyards burned with coal smoke to make the bricks that built the cities north and east, south and west. It was a time between the Great War and the 1930's, when the women knew with gratitude which hours of the day was best to hang out the wash to avoid the ashen smoke of the kilns. Then, young men could hunt in the wooded hills too steep to farm, and they could build secret log cabins on land that did not belong to them. They could pick apples and pears for their families from abandoned trees – their mothers and sisters cooked and canned buckets and bags of them, and legend had it that Johnny Appleseed himself had once walked through this county. If the childless landowner of the hills behind the town ever complained to his wife that the neighborhood boys stole his apples and pears without permission, she scolded him.

"Never mind about that, they have large families and can use the fruit that would just go to waste!"

Almost all were honest in every other way and those that were not were tolerated with a careful consideration. Everyone knew what it was for someone to experience poverty, in this country or the country from which they came, and how little kindness it could take to assuage a bit of it if you could.

The trains used to come through here for the brickyards, and during the hard times the hobos gathered around campfires in a camp away from the railroad siding by the edge of town. More than one housewife would let a man come to the back door for a sandwich and a cup of coffee, if he was nothing but polite.

That was a long time ago.

I leaned over and opened the passenger door for her.

"I can give you a ride, wherever you need to go," I said.

She got into the car, closed the door, and we merged back onto the highway.